Cold Comfort Farm

Stella Gibbons

© Copyright – Stella Gibbons

© Copyright 2008 – BN Publishing

www.bnpublishing.net

info@bnpublishing.net

For information regarding special discounts for bulk purchases,
please contact sales@bnpublishing.net

CONTENTS

1 Flora Poste..1

2 First impressions of Cold Comfort Farm.................13

3 Flora starts tidying up...22

4 Reuben, Seth, and Amos...33

5 Mr Mybug falls in love..46

6 Help for Reuben and Elfine.....................................54

7 The Hawk-Monitor Ball...67

8 The Counting...78

9 Seth's departure...87

10 Judith and Aunt Ada...97

11 Elfine's wedding...108

SUSSEX DIALECT...119

GLOSSARY..120

1

Flora Poste

The education given to Flora Poste by her parents had been too expensive, too full of team sports, and too long. So when they died of a sudden illness within a few weeks of each other, during her twentieth year, Flora was discovered to possess every skill except that of earning enough to live on.

Her father had always been described as a wealthy man, but on his death the lawyers were surprised to find him a poor one. After all the necessary taxes and bills had been paid, his child was left with an income of one hundred pounds a year, and no property.

Flora inherited, however, from her father a strong determination and from her mother an attractive ankle. The first had not been weakened by the fact that she always did what she wanted, nor the second by the violent outdoor sports which she had been forced to play, but she realized that neither was adequate as equipment for finding paid employment.

She decided, therefore, to stay with a friend, a Mrs Mary Smiling, at her house in Lambeth, a fashionable part of London, until she could make up her mind where she and her hundred pounds a year should go.

The death of her parents did not cause Flora much sadness, as she had hardly known them. They had been extremely fond of travelling, and spent only a month or so of each year in England. Flora, from the age of ten, had passed her school holidays at the house of Mary's mother, and when Mary married, Flora spent them at her friend's house instead. She felt, therefore, as if she was returning home when she entered Lambeth, on a dark afternoon in February, a fortnight after her father's funeral.

Mrs Smiling had inherited three houses in Lambeth when her husband died, and now lived in the pleasantest of the three, number 1, Mouse Place, facing the River Thames. One of the others had been sold, and the third had been rented out as a gentlemen's club.

'How glad I am,' she occasionally said to her close friends, 'that poor Tod left me all his property! It *does* bring in such a lot of money.' Like all people who have been disagreeably poor and have become deliciously rich, Mrs Smiling had never grown used to her money, and always took delight in thinking what a lot of it she had. And all her friends looked on with approval, as if she were a nice child with a toy.

Mrs Smiling had two interests in life. One was bringing reason and common sense to the hearts and minds of about fifteen gentlemen of good family and fortune who were madly in love with her, and who had gone to work in such wild and distant places as Jhonsong La Lake M'Luba-M'Luba and the Kwanhattons because of her refusal to marry them. She wrote to them all once a week, and they (as her friends were only too aware, because she was always reading aloud long, boring bits from their letters) wrote to her. These gentlemen were known collectively as 'Mary's Explorers' by her social circle.

Mrs Smiling's second interest was her collection of brassières, and her search for a perfect one. She was said to have the largest and finest collection of this type of underwear in the world. It was hoped that on her death it would be left to the nation. She was an expert on the cut, fit, colour, construction, and proper use of brassières, and her friends had learnt that they could interest or calm her, even in moments of extreme emotion, by saying the following words: 'I saw a brassière today, Mary, that would have interested you . . .'

Mrs Smiling's character was firm and her tastes civilized. Her system of dealing with human nature when it insisted on forcing its coarseness upon her way of life was short and effective: she pretended things were not like that, and usually, after a time, they were not. Certain religions take the same approach; they are perhaps larger organizations, but seldom so successful.

'Of *course*, if you *encourage* people to think they're messy, they *will* be messy,' was one of Mrs Smiling's favourite sayings. Another was, '*Nonsense*, Flora. You *imagine* things.'

'Well, darling,' she said when Flora entered, 'will you have tea or a drink?'

Flora, who was tall, bent and kissed her friend, and said she would have tea. She folded her gloves and put her coat over the back of a chair, and took a cup of tea.

'Was the funeral awful?' asked Mrs Smiling. She knew that Flora did not greatly regret her parents' death.

'It was dreadful,' replied Flora. 'But I must say all the older relations seemed to enjoy it a lot.'

'Did any of them ask you to go and live with them? I meant to warn you about that. Relations are always wanting you to go and live with them,' said Mrs Smiling.

'No. Remember, Mary, I have only a hundred pounds a year now. And I cannot play card games.'

'How *can* people spend their time playing cards?' said Mrs Smiling. 'I think you are very fortunate, darling, to have got through all those awful years at school and college, where you had to play all those terrible outdoor games, without getting to like them yourself. How did you manage it?'

Flora considered. 'Well, first of all I used to stand quite still and stare at the trees and not think about anything. But I found that people *would* bump into me, so I had to give up standing still, and run about like the others. I started running *after* the ball – because that's what's important in a team game, isn't it, Mary? – until I found they didn't like me doing that, because I never got near the ball or hit it or did whatever you are supposed to do with it. So then I ran *away* from it instead, but they didn't seem to like that either.

'And then a whole lot of them told me after one game that I was *no good*. And the games teacher seemed quite worried, and asked me if I really didn't *care* about games, and I said no, I was afraid I didn't, really. And she said it was a pity, because my father was so keen, and what *did* I care about?

'So I said, well, I wasn't quite sure, but on the whole I liked having everything very tidy and calm all round me, and not being asked to do things, and laughing at the kind of joke other people didn't think at all funny, and going for country walks, and not being asked to express *opinions* about things (like love). So then she said, oh, well, didn't I think I could be a little more enthusiastic, because of Father, and I said, no, I was afraid I couldn't, and after that they left me alone.'

Mrs Smiling nodded her approval. She said, 'Now about this

going to live with someone. Of course, you can stay here as long as you like, darling. But I suppose you will want to start some kind of work some time, won't you, and earn enough to have a flat of your own?'

'What kind of work?' asked Flora.

'Well – organizing work, like I used to do.' (Mrs Smiling had been an organizer for a fashionable club before her marriage.) 'Do not ask me what that is exactly, as I've forgotten. It's so long since I did any. But I am sure you could do it. Or you might be a journalist. Or an accountant.'

Flora shook her head. 'I'm afraid I couldn't do any of those things, Mary.'

'Well . . . what then, darling? Now, Flora, don't be *silly*. You know perfectly well that you will be *miserable* if you haven't got a job, when all your friends have. Besides, a hundred pounds a year won't even buy your gloves and underwear. What will you live on?'

'My relations,' replied Flora.

Mrs Smiling looked at her, shocked, as although she was civilized in her tastes, she was a strongminded and moral woman.

'Yes, Mary,' repeated Flora firmly, 'I am only nineteen, but I have already observed that while there is still some foolish prejudice against living on one's friends, it is perfectly respectable to ask one's relations to provide one with a home. Now I am peculiarly (I think if you could see some of them, you would agree that is the correct word) rich in relations, on both sides of the family. There is an unmarried cousin of Father's in Scotland. There is a sister of Mother's at Worthing, on the south coast. A female cousin of Mother's lives in Kensington. And there are also some distant cousins who live in Sussex, I believe . . .'

'Sussex,' murmured Mrs Smiling. 'I don't much like the sound of that. Do they live on some dreadful muddy farm?'

'I am afraid they do,' confessed Flora unwillingly. 'However, I need not try them until all else fails. I propose to send a letter to the relations I have mentioned, explaining the situation and asking if they are ready to give me a home in exchange for my beautiful eyes and a hundred pounds a year.'

'Flora, you must be *mad!*' cried Mrs Smiling. 'Why, you would *die* after the first week. You know that neither of us have ever been able to put up with relations. You must stay here with me, and learn to type, and then you can be somebody's secretary and have a nice little flat of your own, and we can have lovely parties . . .'

'Mary, you know I hate parties. My idea of hell is a very large party in a cold room, where everybody has to play a team game with great enthusiasm. But I was going to say that when I have found a relation who is willing to have me, I shall take him or her in hand, and alter his or her character and way of living to suit my own taste. Then, when it pleases me, I shall marry.'

'Who, tell me?' demanded Mrs Smiling rudely. She was feeling rather upset.

'Somebody whom I shall choose. I have always liked the sound of "a marriage has been arranged". And so it should be arranged! Is it not the most important step a human being can take? That is how my marriage will be.'

Mrs Smiling was horrified at Flora's cold and businesslike attitude. She herself believed that a marriage should be the joining of two loving natures, celebrated in church, with all the usual flowers, music, guests and so on, as her own had been.

'But what I wanted to ask you was,' continued Flora, 'do you think I should write just one letter, and send a copy of it to each relation? Would they be impressed by my efficiency?'

'No,' said Mrs Smiling firmly, 'they would not like that. You must write to them (making it a *completely* different letter each time, Flora), explaining the situation – that is, if you are going to be so mad as to go on with the idea.'

'I will write the letters tomorrow. I think, Mary, we ought to have dinner out tonight – don't you? – to celebrate the beginning of my new life. I will take you to the New River Club!'

'Don't be silly. You know perfectly well we must have some men to go with.'

'Then you can find them. Are any of the Explorers home for a few days?'

'Yes, Bikki is. And your second cousin, Charles Fairford, is in town. The tall, serious, dark one.'

'An excellent choice,' said Flora, with approval. 'He has such a funny little nose.'

Later that evening they all drove away from Mouse Place in Mrs Smiling's car. Bikki was plain and thirtyish, and talked a great deal. Charles spoke very little, but occasionally gave a loud, deep, musical laugh when amused by anything. He was twenty-three and studying for the priesthood. He stared out of the window most of the time, and hardly looked at Flora.

Mrs Smiling was still thinking about her earlier conversation with Flora. 'I shall probably have to come and rescue you,' she said coldly, 'from some impossible relations living in some unreachable place, when you can't bear it any longer. Have you told Charles about it?'

7

'Certainly not! Charles is a relation. He might think I wanted an invitation to go and live with him and his mother.'

'Well, you could live with us if you liked,' said Charles, turning away from the window to look at her. 'Probably Mother and I would quite like it if you did.'

'Don't be silly,' said Mrs Smiling. 'Look – here we are.'

The evening passed pleasantly, as they ate and drank at their table by the river, and danced on the glass floor, looking at the water flowing under their feet. When Flora told Charles of her plan, he was silent at first, and she thought he was shocked, because he *was* very serious. But at last he said, looking amused, 'Well, if you get fed up with it, wherever you are, phone me and I will come and rescue you in my plane.'

'Really, Charles? Do you think a priest *ought* to have a plane?' asked Flora, who was in a foolish mood.

'What has that got to do with it?' said Charles calmly. 'Anyway, you let me know and I will come along.'

Flora promised she would, because she liked Charles, and then they danced some more, and all four sat a long time over coffee, and then it was time to go home.

'Good night, Mary,' said Flora sleepily, as she went upstairs to bed. 'I will write my letters tomorrow.'

Mrs Smiling said, 'Good night, darling.' She added, 'You will have thought better of it by then, I am sure.'

However, at breakfast the next morning Mrs Smiling was shocked to find that Flora was determined to carry out her plan.

'I think it's *terrible*, Flora,' cried Mrs Smiling. 'Do you mean to tell me you don't ever want to work at *anything*?'

'Well, when I am fifty-three or so, I would like to write a book as good as *Persuasion*, but set in modern times, of course. Until then I shall collect material for it. If anyone asks me what I work at, I shall answer, "Collecting material". You know, Mary, I think I have much in common with Jane Austen. She liked everything to be tidy and pleasant and comfortable about her, and so do I. Because otherwise, you see, Mary, people cannot even begin to enjoy life. I cannot *bear messes.*'

'Oh, neither can I,' cried Mrs Smiling. 'If there is one thing I do hate, it is a mess. And I do think you are going to be messy, if you go and live with a lot of distant relations.'

'Well, my mind is made up. I am sure it will be amusing, and I expect there will be a lot of material I can collect. And perhaps some of the relations will have messes in their lives which I can tidy up. You know how untidy lives annoy me. Untidiness is uncivilized.'

The use of this word closed the conversation, as the friends shared a strong dislike for what they called 'uncivilized behaviour'. Flora began to write her letters, taking a certain pride in varying the style in which each letter was written, to suit the character and situation of the person who would receive it. The four letters were posted that afternoon.

When two days had passed, with no reply from any of the relations, Mrs Smiling said, 'I hope none of them will answer. And I only pray, if any of them *do* answer, it won't be those people in Sussex. I think the name's awful – what was it? Judith Starkadder of Cold Comfort Farm!'

'I rather agree with you,' said Flora. 'I think, if I find Cousin Judith has any sons who are named Seth, or Reuben, I shall decide not to go. Highly sexed young men on farms are always called Seth or Reuben, and are such a nuisance. Her husband will probably be called Amos.'

Mrs Smiling said darkly, 'I hope there will be a bathroom.'

'Nonsense, Mary!' cried Flora, turning pale. 'Of course there will be a bathroom. Even in Sussex, there must be . . .'

'We shall see. If you do decide to go, remember to send me a telegram if either of your cousins is called Seth or Reuben, or if you want any extra boots or anything. There is bound to be a lot of mud.'

'Untidiness is uncivilized.'

However, on the third morning, four letters arrived for Flora, and were read over breakfast. Aunt Gwen from Worthing was pleased to offer Flora a home, but Flora would have to share a bedroom with her cousin Peggy. Flora shook her head at this. Mr McKnag from Scotland also offered to shelter Flora under his roof, but feared that it would be a little dull for her in his home, as he was frequently ill and the house was ten kilometres from the nearest village.

'Hopeless,' said Mrs Smiling. But Flora was already reading the third letter. Her mother's cousin from Kensington invited her there, but it would involve sharing a bedroom, this time with a caged bird, an old and much-loved parrot.

The fourth letter was in a dirty, cheap yellow envelope, and written on thin, lined paper in childish, messy handwriting. It said:

Dear Cousin,

So you want your rights at last. Well, I have expected to hear from Robert Poste's child these last twenty years. Child, my man once did your father a great wrong. If you will come to us, I will do my best to put it right; but you must never ask me about it.

We are not like other people, maybe, but there have always been Starkadders at Cold Comfort Farm, and we will do our best to welcome Robert Poste's child.

Child, child, if you come to this doomed house, what is to save you? Perhaps you may be able to help us when our hour comes.

Your affectionate cousin,

Judith Starkadder

Flora and Mrs Smiling were much excited by this unusual letter. They agreed that it sounded by far the most interesting of the four. Mrs Smiling hoped that Flora would soon grow tired of living with her Sussex relations, and return to London, while Flora was fascinated by the mention of her rights, and determined to find out what exactly they were. There were no air connections or express trains to that part of the country, so Flora resigned herself to a long, dull journey on several slow trains.

There was quite a little party to say goodbye to Flora at the station. Two Explorers, keeping a jealous eye on each other, accompanied Mrs Smiling, and Charles came too, with a bunch of spring flowers which he nearly forgot, but put into Flora's hands at the last minute.

'Goodbye,' he said. 'Don't forget to phone me if it gets too much for you, and I'll come and take you away.'

'I won't forget, Charles dear. Thank you very much – although I am quite sure I shall find it very amusing.'

'Goodbye!' cried the Explorers.

'Goodbye, darling!' cried Mrs Smiling, as the train began to move.

'Goodbye. Don't forget to feed the parrot!' shouted Flora, who disliked endless goodbyes, as every civilized traveller must.

'What parrot?' they all shouted back at the departing train, just as they were meant to do.

But they were too far away to hear an answer now, and Flora, giving one last wave to Mrs Smiling, sat back in her seat and opened a fashion magazine for the journey.

2

First impressions of Cold Comfort Farm

The farm lay in the shadow of a cold, windswept hill, not far from the village of Howling, and a little further from the small town of Beershorn. It was surrounded on all sides by rough stone buildings, where the animals were kept – cowsheds for the thin, bony cows, stables for the horses, and a separate, windowless shed, where the huge bull, Big Business, lived alone in warm, damp darkness.

The farmhouse was a long, low building, which had been added to and rebuilt many times during its six-hundred-year history. However, by the time of Flora's visit, there was not much of the original building left, except the tradition that it had always been there, and it was not a convenient house to live in. The front door was never used as it led directly into a muddy field. Instead, the family always went in and out of the back door, which opened on to the farmyard facing the cowsheds. Sunlight always took a long time to reach the yard, so it was often in shadow.

The regular sound of milk against metal came from the foul-smelling cowsheds. A bucket was held between Adam Lambsbreath's knees, and his old grey head rested against the side of one of the cows, whose name was Careless. As he milked her, his fingers moved mechanically, and a strange low sound, mindless as the wind itself, came from his lips. He was asleep. He had been awake all night, wandering in thought over the bare shoulders of the hills after his wild bird, his little flower . . . Elfine. The name, unspoken but musical as flowing water, hung in the thick, damp air.

The three other cows, Pointless, Aimless, and Hopeless, were waiting, with dull eyes and heads held miserably low, to be milked. Suddenly a deep, powerful cry broke the quiet of the morning. The echo rang round the yard, and died sadly away. It was Big Business, waking up to another day, in the steamy darkness of his shed.

The sound woke Adam. He lifted his head and looked round confusedly for a moment. Then slowly his eyes, small and wet and lifeless in his primitive face, lost their terror as he realized that he was in the cowshed, that it was half-past six on a winter morning, and that he was performing the same task he had done at this hour and in this place for the past eighty years.

He stood up, sighing, and went over to Pointless, who was eating Hopeless's tail. Adam, who had lived and worked among dumb creatures for so long that he was almost one of them, took the tail out of Pointless's mouth, and gave her his handkerchief to eat instead. She chewed on it while he was milking her, but as soon as he moved on to Aimless, she spat it out and hid it under her foot. She did not want to hurt the old man's feelings by refusing to eat his present to her. There was a closeness between them, a slow, deep, primitive, silent, earth-loving attachment between Adam and all living creatures; they knew each other's simple needs.

14

Suddenly a shadow fell across the door. At once all the cows lifted their heads, and Adam stood up fearfully.

'Adam,' said the woman who stood in the doorway, 'how many buckets of milk will there be this morning?'

''Tes hard to tell,' replied Adam respectfully.

Judith Starkadder made an impatient movement with her large hands. She was an impressive figure, with black hair falling untidily on to her bitter, beautiful shoulders. 'Well, get as much as you can,' she said lifelessly, as she turned away. 'Mrs Starkadder has been comparing us with other farms in the area, and says we should be producing more.'

Adam said nothing.

'And another thing,' continued Judith, 'you will have to drive down to Beershorn station tonight to meet the six o'clock train. Robert Poste's child is coming to stay with us for a while.'

Adam fell back against Pointless. 'Mun I?' he asked pitifully. 'Mun I, Miss Judith? Oh, don't send me! How can I look into her liddle flower-face, me knowin' what I know? Oh, Miss Judith, I beg 'ee not to send me. Besides,' he added, more practically, ''tes sixty-five years since I last drove the horse and trap, and I might have an accident.'

Judith was already halfway across the yard. She turned slowly to reply. 'No, you must go, Adam. You must forget what you know – as we all must, while she is here. As for the driving, you'd better drive the horse and trap to Howling and back six times this afternoon, to get some practice.'

'Couldn't Master Seth go instead o' me?'

Emotion shook the frozen sadness of her face. She said, low and sharp, 'You remember what happened when he went to meet the new kitchen girl . . . No. You must go.'

15

Adam's eyes, like blind pools of water, suddenly lit up with understanding. He turned back to continue milking Aimless, saying, 'Aye, then I'll go, Miss Judith, to bring Robert Poste's child to Cold Comfort. Aye, 'tes strange, but so 'twill be.'

Judith was no longer listening. She crossed the yard and entered the house by the back door.

In the large kitchen, a miserable fire burned, its smoke rising up the blackened walls, and in the centre of the room was a plain wooden table, darkened by age and dirt, with a few spoons and bowls on it. A pot full of coarse porridge hung over the fire, and, looking moodily down into the pot, stood a tall young man whose riding-boots were splashed with mud, and whose rough shirt was open to the waist. The firelight played on the muscles of his manly chest.

'Well, mother mine,' he said at last, 'here I am, you see. I said I would be in time for breakfast, and I have kept my word.'

His voice had a low, throaty, sexy quality, which added to his attractiveness, despite his outward coarseness. Judith breathed deeply. Her chest, and his, rose and fell. The porridge in the pot also rose and fell, moving like a living thing, keeping time with the human passions above it.

'Dog!' said Judith at last, in a deep, dry voice. 'Coward! Wicked one! Will you *ever* lead a moral life? Who were you with last night? Molly? Or Violet? Or Elizabeth? Seth – my son . . . do you want to break my heart?'

'Yes,' said Seth simply. The porridge rose to the top of the pot, and boiled over into the fire.

Biting back her tears, Judith spooned it back into the pot. While she was doing this, there was a confused noise of voices and boots outside. The men were coming in to breakfast.

There were eleven of them, including five distant cousins of the Starkadders, and two brothers of Amos, Judith's husband. This left only four others who were not members of the family, which explained why the mood among the farm-workers was never exactly cheerful. The Starkadders had a depressing influence on those they came into contact with.

A strong family likeness was visible in the fierce, earth-reddened faces of the seven family members. Micah was the biggest of the cousins. His nephew, Urk, was a small, red, cold-eyed man with pointed ears. Urk's brother, Ezra, looked similar, but with a longer nose. Caraway was a thin, silent man, with some of Seth's animal good looks, which he had passed on to his son, Harkaway, a quiet, nervous young man. Amos's brothers, Luke and Mark, were thickly built, heavy men, who hardly ever said a word.

When they were all sitting down, two shadows darkened the sharp, cold light at the doorway, and Amos Starkadder and his eldest son, Reuben, came into the kitchen. The human passions in them seemed deeply hidden, but the porridge boiled over again.

They all ate breakfast in silence. Judith only pretended to eat her porridge, looking all the time with burning eyes at Seth, as he sat at the other side of the table in the pride of casual manhood, with a good many buttons undone.

Suddenly Amos asked, 'Where's Elfine?'

'She is not up yet,' replied Judith. 'I did not wake her. She's no help to me i' the mornings.'

''Tes a godless habit to lie in bed on a working day,' said Amos angrily, 'and those who do will burn in hell for it! Aye' – his furious blue eyes turned to rest on Seth, who was secretly looking at a packet of art pictures under the table – 'and so will those who have unlawful sex! And so will those' – his eyes moved on to Reuben – 'who are just waitin' and hopin' to step into dead men's shoes.'

Silence returned to the kitchen, and after breakfast all the men

The Starkadders ate breakfast in silence.

went back to working in the fields. Adam, left alone in the kitchen, knew it would be his task to wash the dirty dishes, as the hired girl, Meriam, would not be able to. At any moment the time would come for her to give birth, as the whole of Howling knew, and she would add another child to her shameful family in the small wooden house a field away from the farmhouse. Adam's ancient lips took the shape of a smile. After all, it was February, and soon all the animals and plants would be renewing life. That was Nature's way.

Suddenly something like a brightly coloured bird rushed across the kitchen, in a flash of green skirts and flying gold hair, and danced out through the yard up on to the hill.

Adam turned round violently, dropping and breaking two plates. 'Elfine . . . my liddle bird,' he whispered, starting towards the door. But his whisper was answered by silence. 'My liddle one . . . my darlin' . . .' he murmured. He dropped another plate. It broke. 'Wild as a bird, she is,' he sighed. 'Ah, but if he' – the blind grey pools of his eyes grew suddenly terrible – 'if he harms a hair o' her liddle golden head, I'll *kill* 'un.'

He knew that Elfine was out on the hill, running towards Hightree Hall and the handsome Richard Hawk-Monitor. He imagined, in confused pain, his darling in those casual, uncaring arms . . . Sunk deep in these sorrowful thoughts, he went slowly to the cowshed, and led the cows out to the field. He did not notice that Hopeless's leg had come off, and that she was managing as well as she could with three.

Left alone, the kitchen fire went out.

* * *

As instructed by Judith, Adam arrived at the station in the early evening. Sitting in the trap, he waited, his eyes closed, as still as a sleeping animal. Time had no meaning for him. Instead, the names of Elfine and Richard Hawk-Monitor turned and turned endlessly in his head.

Suddenly he realized that something was happening. The dirt which had been lying on the floor of the trap for the last twenty-five years was being kicked out into the road by a small foot with an attractive ankle. Meanwhile a voice was saying, 'How disgusting!'

'Eh . . . eh,' murmured Adam, looking confusedly into the darkness. 'Is that 'ee, Robert Poste's child?'

'It is,' said Flora. 'Now shall we start, if you are *quite* ready? My luggage will be arriving tomorrow. Would you like me to drive?'

Adam was so shocked by this offer that he started driving immediately. Flora sat next to him, with her coat buttoned up to her neck to protect her from the cold night air, and holding her small overnight bag on her knees. Her journey had been long and rather uncomfortable, and she felt depressed at the thought of what she might find at Cold Comfort. She felt relieved, at least, that at the last moment she had packed her dearly loved copy of *The Thoughts of Father Bertrand*. It would be easier to meet the Starkadders in a proper and civilized way if she were guided by *The Thoughts*.

When they arrived, Flora stepped carefully through the foul-smelling yard, and was met at the door by Judith.

'Oh, how do you do?' said Flora politely. 'You must be my cousin Judith. Terribly nice of you to have me. Isn't it strange we have never met?' She put out her hand, but Judith did not take it at once. The seconds passed while the older woman stared into Flora's face in silence.

'Have I got a dirty mark on my nose?' Flora wondered. And then she realized what was happening. It was the first time a Starkadder had ever looked upon a civilized being.

'Will you think me awfully rude, Cousin Judith,' said Flora eventually, 'if I do not meet the rest of the family this evening? Might I just possibly have a light supper in my room?'

'It is cold there,' said Judith, heavily, at last.

'Oh, a fire will soon warm the room,' said Flora firmly. 'So nice of you, I do think, to take care of me.'

'My sons, Seth and Reuben' – Judith swallowed, then continued in a lower voice – 'my sons are waiting to see you.'

'How nice of them,' said Flora, smiling sweetly, 'but I think, all the same, I will see them in the morning. Shall we go in? Oh, and I would like Adam to send this telegram for me.' Quickly she wrote a note and gave it to Judith.

Half an hour later, she sat beside a smoky fire in her room, eating two boiled eggs, which had seemed the safest thing to ask for. She was thinking that if the dusty corridors, the unused rooms and the ancient furniture were typical of the house, and Judith and Adam were typical of the Starkadders, her task at Cold Comfort would be long and difficult. However, she refused to admit defeat, and return, beaten, to London, otherwise Mrs Smiling might say, 'I told you so.'

And indeed, far away in Mouse Place, Mrs Smiling was at that moment reading with some satisfaction a telegram saying:

WORST FEARS REALIZED DARLING. SETH AND REUBEN TOO.
SEND BOOTS.

3

Flora starts tidying up

She was woken very early next morning by a noisy quarrel going on below her window. Male voices were raised in anger.

'Hopeless has lost a leg! Where is it, ye old fool?'

'I don't know, Master Reuben. An' if I did, I wouldn't tell 'ee.' Flora thought she recognized that high, ancient voice.

'But who'll buy her now when I take her to Beershorn market? Who wants a cow wi' only three legs?'

'Don't speak like that about our Hopeless, Master Reuben! Shame on 'ee, countin' every mouthful o' grass th' cows eat! Who should know the dumb creatures better than me? I know what's in their hearts, but I don't watch 'em from morning till night to see where they leave their legs!'

'Now, listen to me, Adam Lambsbreath—'

At this point Flora got crossly out of bed and felt her way across the dark room to the window. She pushed it open and called down, 'I say, *would* you mind not talking quite so loudly please? I *am* so sleepy, and I would be *so* grateful if you would be a little quieter.' Total silence followed her request, and she went back to sleep.

When she woke again, it was daylight, and her watch said it

22

was half-past eight. There was not a sound from the yard or from anywhere in the old house. Everybody might have died in the night.

'Not a hope of hot water, of course,' thought Flora. But she was pleased to find that the water was soft, so she did not mind washing in cold water. She looked round her room while she was dressing, and decided she liked it. It was large and unusually high, with old, heavy furniture, and two beautiful, old-fashioned mirrors. The curtains were of excellent quality, but rather dirty. 'They must be washed today,' Flora told herself.

She went downstairs, finding her way with difficulty through the dark corridors. A smell of burnt porridge floated up from the kitchen, and she noticed a breakfast tray outside one of the bedrooms. 'Good,' she thought. 'If someone else has breakfast in their room, then so can I, another time.'

Eventually she found the kitchen, which at first seemed empty. The door leading into the yard was open, and a cold wind was blowing in. Flora went across and shut the door firmly.

'Eh, never do that, Robert Poste's child!' protested a voice from the back of the kitchen, near the sink. 'I cannot cletter the dishes and watch the dumb creatures in the cowshed at the same time, if ye shut the door.'

Flora recognized old Adam. 'I am sorry,' she said clearly, 'but I cannot eat breakfast in a cold room. *Is* there any breakfast, by the way?'

Adam came slowly forward into the light. Flora wondered if he ever washed. 'There's porridge, Robert Poste's child.'

'I don't much care for porridge. Is there any bread and butter? And some tea? And have you a piece of clean newspaper to cover the table with? There's porridge all over it!'

23

'There's tea and bread and butter over there. Ye mun find 'em yourself, Robert Poste's child. I have my tasks to do, and I cannot run here and there to serve a young thing like 'ee. Besides, we've troubles enough at Cold Comfort without bringin' in a newspaper to upset and frighten us.'

'Oh, have you? What troubles?' asked Flora interestedly, as she busily made some tea. This seemed a good opportunity to learn something about the other members of the family. 'Haven't you enough money? Is that the problem?'

'There's money enough i' the farm, Robert Poste's child, but the seeds do not grow and the animals have no young ones. An' why? Because there's a *curse* on us, Robert Poste's child.'

'But, look here, couldn't something be done about it? – (This bread is really not at all bad, you know. Surely you don't bake it here?) – Perhaps Cousin Amos could sell the farm, and buy another, without any curse on it, somewhere else?'

Adam shook his head. 'Nay, there've always been Starkadders at Cold Comfort. There's reasons why we can't leave. Mrs Starkadder, she says we've got to stay here. 'Tes her whole life, 'tes her life's blood, Cold Comfort.'

'Cousin Judith, you mean? But she doesn't seem very happy here.'

'Nay, Robert Poste's child, I mean the old lady.' His voice sank to a whisper, and he looked respectfully upwards.

'Is she dead, then?' asked Flora, thinking Adam must mean that old Mrs Starkadder was in heaven.

Adam laughed. It was a strange, dry sound. 'Nay, she's alive, all right. Her hand lies on us like iron, Robert Poste's child. But she never leaves her room, and she never sees anyone except Miss Judith.'

24

He stopped suddenly, as if he had said too much, and turned back to the sink. 'I mun cletter th' dishes now. Leave me i' peace, Robert Poste's child.'

'Oh, all right. But I do wish you would call me Miss Poste. Or even Flora. I do feel that "Robert Poste's child" every time is rather a mouthful, don't you?'

'Leave me i' peace. I mun cletter th' dishes.'

Flora said no more, but thoughtfully finished her breakfast. 'So that's the answer!' she was thinking. 'Old Mrs Starkadder is the curse of Cold Comfort! She must be Aunt Ada Doom.' Flora sighed. She knew that old ladies like Aunt Ada took great delight in arguing and interfering, and she was sure that if she intended to tidy up life at Cold Comfort, she would find herself opposed by the influence of Aunt Ada.

She felt more cheerful when she remembered that, in addition to Father Bertrand's *Thoughts*, she had brought with her a copy of *The Higher Common Sense*, by the same author. *The Thoughts* were helpful with everyday, routine difficulties, but *The Higher Common Sense* provided a guide for civilized people facing a really serious problem of the Aunt Ada kind.

On the whole, Cold Comfort was not without its promise of mystery and excitement, and she wished that Charles was there to share it with her. Charles really enjoyed a mystery.

Meanwhile, Adam had brought a small stick in from the yard, turned on the cold tap, and started scratching at the cold dried porridge on the plates. Flora could hardly believe her eyes, but waited as long as she could before saying, 'Surely you could do that much more easily with a little mop? A nice little mop with a handle? It would get the dishes cleaner, and save a lot of time.'

'I don't want a liddle mop wi' a handle. I've used a stick for

25

fifty years and more, and what was good enough then is good enough now. An' I don't want to cletter the dishes more quickly. It passes th' time, and takes my thoughts off my liddle wild Elfine.'

'But,' suggested Flora cleverly, remembering the conversation that had woken her early that morning, 'if you had a little mop and could wash the dishes more quickly, you could have more time in the cowshed with the dumb creatures.'

Adam stopped his work, evidently impressed by this.

Flora added quickly, 'Anyway, I shall buy one for you when I go to Beershorn tomorrow.'

At this moment, the door opened and a figure in a long green dress rushed across the room and up the stairs so rapidly that Flora hardly saw it.

'Who was that?' she asked.

'My darlin', my liddle Elfine,' said Adam.

'Indeed, and does she always rush about like that?' enquired Flora coldly. She considered her cousin lacking in politeness.

'Aye, she's as wild an' shy as th' birds i' the trees. She's away from home all day, wanderin' over th' hills. Aye, an' at night too . . .' His face grew angry. 'Aye, at night she wanders far from those that love her. She'll break my old heart, she will.'

'Does she go to school? How old is she?'

'She's seventeen. Nay, never talk o' school for my Elfine, Robert Poste's child. Ye might as well send a flower to school as her. She learns from th' skies an' the wild birds, not out o' books.'

'Oh, does she!' observed Flora, who was feeling lonely and rather cross. 'Now, where *is* everybody this morning? I want to see Miss Judith before I go out for a walk.'

'Master Amos and Master Reuben are scranletting th' fields

with th' men, Master Seth is off mollocking somewhere in the village, and Miss Judith is layin' out th' cards upstairs.'

'Well, I shall go and find her. What does mollocking mean? No, you need not tell me. I can guess. What time is lunch? And – er – who cooks it?'

'One o'clock, Robert Poste's child. And Miss Judith, she cooks th' lunch. Were ye afraid *I* would cook it?'

Flora *had* in fact been worried about that, and was glad to hurry away from his accusing stare. But it was a relief to know she would be able to eat the lunch. She had been prepared to starve rather than eat anything cooked by Adam.

She had no idea where Judith's bedroom might be, but soon found a guide to take her there. On the stairs she met the girl in green running lightly down. Elfine stopped, as though shot, at the sight of Flora. 'Pretending to be a wild bird again,' thought Flora, while giving her a pleasant smile.

'What do you want?' whispered Elfine.

'Cousin Judith's bedroom,' replied Flora. '*Would* you mind showing me the way? It's *so* easy to get lost in a strange house, isn't it?' She noticed that her cousin's eyes were large, blue, and very fine, but that her dress was the wrong green.

'Do forgive me,' she said smoothly, 'but I would love to see you in blue. Those dull greens are so very difficult, I always think. If I were you, I'd try blue – something *really* well cut, of course, and very simple – but it must be blue. Try it, and see.'

Elfine did not answer this. She said casually, 'Here it is,' as they arrived in front of a closed door.

'Thank you so much,' said Flora charmingly. Elfine gave her a long stare, then rushed off down the corridor. 'I will have to start work on her at once,' thought Flora. 'In another year it will be too late, because even if she escapes from this place, she will only go and open a café in some seaside town, and try to look artistic in long flowery skirts and open-toed shoes.'

And sighing a little at the greatness of the task she had given herself, Flora knocked at the door and went in.

Two hundred photographs of Seth, aged from six weeks to twenty-four years, stared down from the walls of the bedroom. Judith was sitting with some dirty-looking cards laid out on the table in front of her. The bed was not made. Nor had she brushed her hair, which hung around her face like lifeless black snakes.

'Good morning,' said Flora brightly. 'I'm so sorry to interrupt you if you are busy. I just wanted to know if you would like me to amuse myself, or if you wanted to make other arrangements for me. Personally, I think it's much easier if a guest finds her own way of passing the time. I am sure you are much too busy to want to bother with looking after me.'

Judith, after a long stare at her younger cousin, threw back her head with its load of snakes. Her laugh rang unpleasantly through the cold air.

'Busy! Busy waiting to die, you mean. Nay, do what you please, Robert Poste's child, as long as you don't interrupt my loneliness. Give me time, and I will put right the wrong that my man did to your father. Give . . . us . . . all . . . time . . .' – the words came slowly and unwillingly.

'I suppose,' suggested Flora politely, 'you would not care to tell me what the wrong was? I do feel it would make matters easier . . .'

Judith pushed away the words with a heavy movement of her hand, like an animal in pain. 'Haven't I told you my lips are sealed?'

'Just as you like, Cousin Judith. Now I hope you don't mind my mentioning money, but I would like to ask you when I should pay you for my food and living expenses. You know I have a hundred pounds a year of my own.'

'Keep it – keep it,' said Judith violently. 'We will never touch Robert Poste's money. While you are here, you are the guest of Cold Comfort.'

'How very kind,' said Flora, who was privately rather annoyed. If she lived at Cold Comfort as a guest, it would be extremely rude of her to interfere in the family's way of life, but if she paid for herself, she could interfere as much as she liked. 'Another thing, Cousin Judith,' she added. 'I simply love my bedroom, but do you think I could have the curtains washed? I believe they are red, and I would so like to make sure.'

'Curtains?' asked Judith vacantly. She seemed to have fallen into a dream. 'Child, child, it is many years since we have washed curtains at Cold Comfort. Adam's old arms are not strong enough. I suppose Meriam, the hired girl, might, but—'

She looked out of the window at a small wooden house at the far end of the field, and a slow wave of blood flooded her face. 'I heard her cries of pain,' she whispered thickly. 'She has given birth. 'Tes the fourth love-child she has had! The fourth! Every year, in the fullness of summer, when the sukebind hangs heavy from the branches, 'tes the same. 'Tes the hand of Nature, and we women cannot escape it.'

'Oh, can't we?' thought Flora. But aloud she said, 'Well, she can't wash the curtains if she's just had a baby, can she?'

'Such girls are like field animals,' said Judith. 'She'll be working again tomorrow. You can ask her if you wish.' She seemed weighed down by some great sorrow, and as she spoke, she looked angrily across the room at a photograph of Seth in football clothes.

'He is really very handsome,' thought Flora, following Judith's glance. 'I don't suppose he plays football any more – he probably mollocks instead.'

'Aye,' whispered Judith suddenly, 'look at him – the shame of our house. A curse on the day he was born, and a curse on his silver tongue, that leads weak women to shame and ruin.' She stood up and looked out into the steady rain.

Flora realized that the conversation was not likely to develop beyond this point, so she rose, said goodbye, and left Judith to her bitter thoughts.

'So Seth is the father of all Meriam's children,' thought Flora. 'Really, it is too bad. I must see what I can do about Seth.'

That afternoon, she visited Meriam's small house, and was relieved to find that the girl had recovered so quickly from giving birth that she was reading a magazine and looking bored. Flora introduced herself and asked after Meriam's health.

'And if you feel well enough,' she went on, 'I would like you to wash my bedroom curtains.'

Meriam was doubtful. 'Haven't I enough to do, wi' three children to feed, and my mother lookin' after a fourth? And who's to know what will happen to me when the sukebind is out again, on th' long summer evenings—'

'Nothing will happen to you,' said Flora, 'if only you use your intelligence. Listen.' And carefully, she explained in some detail how Meriam's recent experience could easily be avoided in future.

Meriam was horrified. ''Tes wickedness! 'Tes going against Nature!' she cried fearfully.

'Nonsense!' said Flora firmly. 'Nature is all right in many ways, but must not be allowed to make things untidy. Now remember, Meriam, no more sukebind and summer evenings without some preparations first. And if you wash my bedroom curtains for me, I will pay you, and that will help to feed your children.'

At that moment the door opened to reveal Meriam's mother, Mrs Beetle. Her sharp little black eyes examined Flora with interest. 'Good morning, miss. A nasty wet day,' she said, closing a large umbrella.

Flora was so surprised that anyone in Sussex should speak to her in a respectful and normal manner, that she almost forgot to answer. But habit is strong, and she agreed pleasantly that it was, indeed, a nasty day.

It soon became clear that Mrs Beetle was an admirable character – someone who was very close to being an ordinary human being, and who understood that curtains must be washed and life generally tidied up before anyone could even begin to think of enjoying it.

'Meriam'll wash your curtains for you, and I'll come an' collect them myself, miss, with pleasure,' said Mrs Beetle, as she quickly tidied up the small room. 'About time someone did some washing at Cold Comfort. That old Adam could do with a wash himself. *I'm* lookin' after my daughter's children, you know, miss. Well, someone's got to, poor little things. But I've got a plan for them, you see. I'm goin' to turn the four of them into a jazz band. They can earn as much as six pounds a night playing in a London club! So I'm givin' them plenty of milk, and makin' sure they go to bed early. They'll need to be fit and healthy if they're goin' to stay up late playing in night-clubs.'

31

Flora was a little shocked at Mrs Beetle's plan for making money, but felt that at least it was *organized*. She said a pleasant goodbye to Meriam and her mother, and returned to the farmhouse.

As soon as Flora had gone, Meriam told her mother, in a thick whisper, the advice the young lady had given her.

'So that's how it's done!' said Mrs Beetle.

''Tes wickedness,' said Meriam heavily.

'That's right,' said her mother. There was a pause. Then she added, 'All the same, it might be worth tryin'.'

4

Reuben, Seth, and Amos

By lunch-time the next day, the endless rain, the dusty, dirty farmhouse, and her truly awful relations had made Flora feel quite depressed, which was as unusual as it was unpleasant. She decided, therefore, to cheer herself up by walking to the village to find a pub to have lunch in. Then she would return to the farm to meet all her cousins at tea-time. So far she had not met any of the male Starkadders or Aunt Ada. 'I'll prepare tea myself,' she thought, 'and tell them I intend to do so every afternoon. They probably aren't used to anything so civilized.'

However, when Flora arrived at the bar of the Murdered Man, the only pub in Howling, she discovered that they did not offer lunches except to residents. Fortunately, she was able to persuade the owner's wife, Mrs Murther, to cook an extra piece of meat for her, and in a surprisingly short time was sitting down to enjoy a plate of chicken and vegetables.

'Have you got everything you need, miss?' asked Mrs Murther. 'Now I must go and see to my other visitor's lunch. He's stayin' here. A writer, he is.'

'What's his name?' asked Flora. She wondered if she knew him.

'Mr Mybug,' was the improbable answer.

Flora simply did not believe this, but she was too busy eating to start a long and exhausting argument. She decided Mr Mybug must be extraordinarily clever. Any normal person with a name like that would have changed it by now.

'What a nuisance!' she thought. 'Haven't I got enough to do at Cold Comfort, without having an intellectual called Mybug staying in the village? He will probably fall in love with me. Intellectuals rarely choose women of their own type, but concentrate on normal, quiet, properly dressed people like me.' She finished her meal more quickly than she intended, in case Mr Mybug should come in.

'Don't worry, he's never in before half-past two,' said Mrs Murther kindly, reading her thoughts.

So Flora paid for her lunch, and walked back to the farm, feeling more cheerful. There were sounds of life in the cowshed, and the loud bellow of the bull came from his dark shed. ('I don't believe he's ever let out into the fields when the sun's shining,' thought Flora, and made a note to deal with this, as well as the Starkadders.) Angry noises came from the chicken house, but nobody was visible. She decided to spend a quiet afternoon in her room, arranging her books.

At four o'clock she came downstairs, added more wood to the fire, and put some water in a pot to boil. There was bread and butter, but no cake or anything as lady-like as that. Just as she poured the hot water into the teapot, a shadow darkened the doorway. There stood Reuben, looking at her preparations with an expression of amazement and anger.

'Hullo,' said Flora quickly, to prevent him speaking first. 'I feel sure you must be Reuben. I'm Flora Poste, your cousin, you

34

know. How do you do? Do sit down. Will you have tea? Do you take milk? Sugar?'

Reuben said nothing. His head was full of confused thoughts and questions he could not answer. A woman . . . Had she come to take away his land, the land that would be his when his father died? The land he loved, the dark earth of the fields under rain, the swelling of seeds into green plants, the smell and cry of cows . . . They were his, all his . . .

'Here is your tea,' said Flora. 'Do have some bread and butter. Oh, never mind your boots. Adam can sweep up the mud afterwards. Do come in.'

Defeated, Reuben came in.

He stood at the table, staring at Flora and blowing heavily on his tea to cool it. Flora did not mind. It was quite interesting, like having tea with a bull. Besides, she was rather sorry for him. Of all the Starkadders, he seemed to enjoy life the least. Amos had religion, Judith had Seth, Adam had his dumb creatures, Elfine danced about on the hills in a peculiar green dress, and Seth went mollocking. But poor Reuben didn't seem to have any such interests.

After a silence which lasted seven minutes by Flora's watch, Reuben finally produced the following remark: 'I scranletted five o' th' fields today.'

'Did you?' said Flora, in a bright, interested way. She saw immediately that she had said the wrong thing. How awful! He thought she did not believe him!

'Aye, I did too. Five fields, without a man to help me. Could ye have done that, I'd like to know?'

'No, indeed,' said Flora warmly. 'But then, you see, I wouldn't want to.'

35

This innocent confession had a surprising effect on Reuben. He pushed his face forward, staring fiercely into hers.

'Wouldn't you, then? Ah, but you'd pay a hired man good money to do it for you – wastin' the farm's profits.'

Flora was now beginning to see what was the matter. He thought that she wanted to take over the farm!

'I scranletted five o' th' fields today.'

'Indeed I wouldn't,' she replied quickly. 'I wouldn't care if the fields weren't scranletted at all.' She smiled pleasantly at him. 'I'd let you do it.'

Again she had chosen the wrong thing to say. 'Let!' he shouted, banging on the table. 'Let! What a word to use to a man who has looked after this farm as a father looks after his child! Let – aye, a fine word—'

'I really think I had better explain things,' interrupted Flora. 'I don't want the farm. Really, I don't. In fact' – she hesitated whether she should tell him it seemed unbelievable to her that anyone could possibly want it, but decided this would be rude as well as unkind – 'I know nothing about farming, and would much rather leave it to people like you, who do. You must see that I am the last person in the world who would be any use at scranletting. I'm sure you will believe me.'

The expression on Reuben's face was changing, but he did not reply. He banged his cup down on the table and went out, with a last stare at Flora. She felt fairly satisfied with their conversation, and hoped that he was beginning to believe that she had no intention of taking over the farm.

She sat down quietly by the fire, and picked up some underwear she was mending. Suddenly a young man, who could only be Seth, came in.

Flora looked up with a cool smile. 'How do you do? Are you Seth? I'm your cousin, Flora Poste. I'm afraid you're too late for any tea . . . unless you'd like to make a fresh pot of it.'

He came over to her, moving like a wild and beautiful animal, and stood close, looking down at her. Flora saw at once that he was not the kind to be interested in offers of tea.

'What's that you're makin'?' he asked.

37

Flora knew that he hoped it was a brassière. 'Just a small cloth for the tea-table,' she replied calmly.

'Aye ... woman's nonsense,' said Seth softly. 'Women are all alike, always makin' a fuss over this an' that, makin' men look at 'em, when all they really want is man's blood an' his heart out o' his body an' his soul an' his pride ...'

'Really?' said Flora, looking in her sewing-box for her scissors.

'Aye. That's all women want – a man's life. Then when they've got him tied up in their women's ways and their softness, do ye know what they do then?'

'I'm afraid not,' said Flora. 'Would you mind passing me that needle and cotton, just behind you? Thank you so much.' Seth passed it mechanically, and continued.

'They eat him. That's what women do, if a man lets 'em. But I – I don't let women eat me. I eat them instead.'

Flora thought that silence was the best response to this. After all, his conversation was just a kind of game, a little battle of words in which each player tried to score points. It was a game that Flora was familiar with (from parties in London and elsewhere). And as, in her case, one of the players was a little bored by it all and was just looking forward to some hot milk before going to bed that night, there was not much point in playing.

However, she did not want to appear rude, so she smiled up at him and said, 'I am sure that is very interesting. Now tell me, what do you do on the evenings when you aren't – er – eating people?'

'I go to Beershorn,' said Seth. 'I go to th' cinema there.'

And something in the way he said it made Flora put down her

sewing and look thoughtfully at his handsome face. 'So, you like films?'

'Better than anything else in th' whole world,' he said fiercely. 'Better than Mother, or th' farm, or women. I've got photos of every film star there's ever been. I can tell you their names, I know their voices, I know all about 'em.' Talking about the passion of his life made him sound almost human.

'Indeed,' said his cousin, still looking at him thoughtfully. 'That's interesting. Very interesting indeed.'

But she said nothing of the plan that had come to her in a flash, and Seth suddenly decided he had been betrayed into talking to a woman about something else than love, and was angry. So he went out of the kitchen, into the yard, leaving Flora to a quiet evening on her own.

All this was pleasant enough. She had made a good start at tidying up Cold Comfort, although she had only been there for two days. But soon she must get to know the rest of the Starkadders, and that unfortunately would involve taking some of her meals with them.

But it was not easy getting to meet all the family. Another whole week passed, and still no one suggested introducing her to Aunt Ada Doom. Flora watched, fascinated, as Mrs Beetle, who came regularly to help in the kitchen, took heavily loaded trays of food up to Aunt Ada's room, and later brought them down empty.

Once Flora said casually, 'I have not met my aunt yet.'

'You haven't missed much, Miss Poste,' said Mrs Beetle darkly. 'But she's the only one here that knows her own mind, even if she did see something nasty in the woodshed when she was two.'

Flora had no idea what she meant, but was not the type of person who questions servants, and so no more was said on the matter.

Meanwhile, there was Amos. She had discovered from Adam that Amos preached twice a week to the Church of the Shaking Brothers, a religious group which met in Beershorn. She decided to accompany him one evening, and begin working on him during the long drive to the town.

So, on the Thursday evening of her second week at the farm, she approached her cousin and said firmly, 'Are you going to Beershorn to preach to the Brothers tonight?'

Amos looked hard at her. 'Aye,' he said, in a satisfied voice, after a pause. 'They'll all burn in hell, and I mun surely tell 'em so.'

'Well, may I come too?'

He did not seem surprised. 'Aye, ye can come, ye poor miserable creepin' sinner. Maybe ye think ye can escape the fires of hell if ye come wi' me and bow down wi' the rest, but 'tes too late! Ye'll burn wi' all the other wicked sinners! Ye'll have to say what your sins have been.'

'Do I have to say them out loud?' asked Flora, a little nervously. She had heard of a similar custom from friends of hers who were being educated at that great centre of religious life, Oxford University.

'Aye, but not tonight. Nay, there'll be too many saying their sins aloud tonight. There'll be no time for the Lord to listen to a new sheep like you. And maybe the spirit won't move ye to speak.'

Flora was fairly sure it would not; so she went upstairs to put on her hat and coat. When she came down, Amos was waiting for her in the horse and trap. It was a cold night, and Flora hesitated.

'Is there a blanket or anything?' she asked.

'Nay. The sins burnin' in your bones will keep 'ee warm.'

But Flora thought otherwise, and went to fetch an extra coat.

They started on their journey and at first Amos was silent. This was typical of the Starkadders, none of whom had any general conversation. But this was a golden opportunity for Flora, who took it.

'It must be so interesting to preach to the Brothers, Cousin Amos,' she said. 'Do you prepare what you're going to say before, or do you just make it up as you go along?'

There was a pause. The figure of Amos, sitting beside her in the darkness, appeared to be swelling with anger, and Flora was quite relieved when he replied in a more or less controlled way.

'Don't speak o' the Lord's word in that godless way. 'Tes no story ye invent to tell children. It is not prepared before – it falls on my mind, straight from heaven.'

'Really! How interesting. Does anyone else preach, or are you the only one?'

'Only me. Deborah Checkbottom tried once to get up and preach. But she couldn't. I knew there'd been a mistake, and the spirit meant for me had fallen on Deborah. So I just hit her with the Lord's good book, to let the devil out of her soul.'

'And did the devil come out?' asked Flora, trying with some difficulty to show the proper spirit of serious enquiry.

'Aye, it came out. We heard no more o' Deborah tryin' to preach. Now I preach alone. No one else gets the word like I do.' He sounded rather pleased with himself. 'O' course, I don't enjoy it. But 'tes my duty, to tell the Brothers, and Sisters' – and here he fixed Flora with a meaningful stare – 'o' the flames of hell fire that will burn 'em for ever.'

Flora suddenly had a very good idea. 'You ought to spread the word wider than the Brothers,' she said. 'You mustn't waste yourself on a few miserable sinners in Beershorn, you know. Why don't you buy a Ford van, and go round the country, preaching on market days?' She was sure that Amos would object to some of the changes she was planning to make to the farm, so it would be much easier for her to get things done, if he were out of the way on a long preaching tour.

Amos obviously found her suggestion appealing. After a long silence he said, 'Aye, there's some truth in what ye say. Maybe it *is* my duty to look for a wider field. I mun think about it.'

'Just think of the *thousands* of sinners whose souls you could save,' urged Flora.

'A Ford van,' Amos murmured to himself. 'Thousands of sinners. Aye, there's something in it.'

At that moment they arrived outside a small building next to the pub in Beershorn High Street. Flora watched with interest as the Brothers (and Sisters) hurried inside to take their seats. When Amos judged that almost everyone had arrived, he said, ''Tes nearly full. We mun go in,' and in they went.

Flora took a seat at the end of a row near the exit, in case she felt like leaving early. A song was sung, to remind the Brothers of their name. It went something like this:

Whatever shall we do, O Lord,
When the wind blows over sea and lake,
When sun beats down on stone and board,
The earth may burn, but we will shake.

Then everyone crossed their legs and arranged themselves

more comfortably, while Amos rose with terrifying slowness and went to stand in front of the rows of seats. For some three minutes he stared at the Brothers, his face wearing an expression of the deepest hatred, mixed with a godlike sorrow and pity. It was an excellent performance, Flora thought approvingly. The man was an artist.

At last he spoke. His voice cracked the silence like a broken bell. 'Ye miserable crawling insects, are ye here again? Have ye come creeping secretly out of your doomed houses to hear o' your punishment? Have ye come to hear me tell ye o' the great red flames o' hell fire?'

A long and effective pause, and another furious stare. Amos continued, with a short laugh, 'Aye, ye've come. And what good will it do ye?' Another pause. 'No good at all.' He drew a long breath, then suddenly shouted out as loudly as he could, '*Ye're all damned!*'

An expression of extreme interest and satisfaction passed over the Brothers' faces, as they coughed and moved about a little in their chairs, making themselves as comfortable as possible while listening to the bad news.

'Damned,' he repeated, his voice sinking to a thrilling and effective whisper. 'Do ye ever stop to think about what that word means? Well, I'll tell ye. It means, that as soon as ye leave this miserable world, ye will go down into the flames of hell, and will burn there for ever and ever, till the end of time.'

He stopped to drink from a glass of water, then began again.

'Ye know, don't ye, what it feels like when ye burn your hand wi' a match? 'Tes a fearful pain, isn't it? And ye hurry to put a bit o' butter on it to take th' pain away. Ah, but' (an impressive pause) '*there'll be no butter in hell!* Your whole body will be

43

burnin' wi' that unbearable pain, and your eyes will be beatin' in your head like great red-hot balls of fire. Your tongue will go black, and your skin will crack an' fall off, and all around ye will be the screams of your nearest and dearest—'

'There'll be no butter in hell!'

It was at this point that Flora rose quietly and walked rapidly to the door. The details of Amos's description and the airlessness of the room made her feel she could pass the evening more profitably elsewhere. But where? There was the cinema, where 'Other Wives' Sins' was showing, but she thought she had heard quite enough about sin for one evening. She looked up and down the street, and noticed a teashop a few doors away. She crossed the road and went in.

No sooner had she entered than she realized that she had gone out of hell fire into an evening of boredom. Sitting at one of the tables, was someone she recognized. She had met him at a party in London, given by a Mrs Polswett. And he could only be Mr Mybug. There was no one else in the teashop. He had a clear field, and she could not escape.

5

Mr Mybug falls in love

He looked up at her as she came in and smiled. By now Flora was really cross. Surely she had put up with enough for one evening without having to listen to intelligent conversation! So she sat down at a table with her back to the supposed Mr Mybug, and hoped for the best.

A waitress brought her coffee, a piece of cake and an orange. Flora drank her coffee, ate her cake and started putting sugar on her orange. Suddenly she heard a voice behind her.

'Hullo, Flora Poste. Do you believe that women have souls?' And there he was, standing at her side and smiling down at her.

She knew that intellectuals always talked like this. So she replied pleasantly, but from her heart, 'I am afraid I am not very interested.'

Mr Mybug laughed. 'Aren't you? Good girl. We'll be all right if only you'll be honest with me. As a matter of fact, I'm not very interested in whether they have souls either. Bodies matter more than souls. You do remember me, don't you? We met at Mrs Polswett's. May I sit here?'

'Do,' said Flora, seeing there was no escape.

Now Mr Mybug was able to concentrate on Flora. He leaned

his elbows on the table, sank his chin in his hands, and looked steadily at her. 'Well?' he said. Flora, with a sinking heart, recognized this behaviour. It was what intellectuals who had decided to fall in love often did.

'You are writing a book, aren't you?' she said, rather quickly. 'Isn't it about Branwell Brontë? I remember Mrs Polswett mentioning it to me.'

'Yes, that's right. For far too long people have believed the old story about the Brontë sisters writing all those wonderful novels.' He glanced quickly at Flora to see if she looked surprised or shocked, but the gentle, interested expression on her face did not change, so he continued. 'You see, it's obvious that their brother, Branwell, wrote them all – the quality of the writing is so *male* – and his sisters hated him because he was such a great writer.'

'I thought most of the documents of the time show that his sisters loved him dearly,' said Flora, only too pleased to keep their conversation impersonal.

'I know, but that was just their clever little game, you see. They were extremely jealous of him, but they dared not show it. They wanted to keep him at home, where they could steal his work and sell it as their own, to buy more alcohol.'

'Who for – Branwell?'

'No, for themselves. They all drank heavily. Poor Branwell used to have to go to the pub to ask for alcohol for his sisters – that's why people always thought *he* was the drinker! What a wonderful, loving brother he was, caring so little for his own reputation! I've proved all this, using three letters I've discovered, written by Branwell to an old aunt living in Ireland.'

'Are you sure he really wrote these letters?' asked Flora. In her

47

personal experience, it was not the habit of artists and poets to take time to write to old aunts; this task, indeed, was usually performed by their wives or sisters.

'Oh, absolutely. You see, his aunt was the passion of his life,' said Mr Mybug simply. 'For him, she was mystery . . . woman . . . the unsolvable question, the unfindable answer. In his letters we can read his passion between the lines. He asks how is her health . . . has her cat recovered from his illness . . . what is the weather like . . . how is Cousin Martha (and what a picture we get of Martha in these simple words).'

Flora glanced at her watch. It was half-past eight. She could hear the Brothers singing across the road. She hoped that soon they would be released, and she would be able to leave.

Mr Mybug was still looking steadily at her, and now he said, 'Do you care about walking?'

She now had a dreadful choice to make. If she said she loved walking, Mr Mybug would take her out all day in the rain while he talked about sex, and if she said that she only quite liked it, he would make her sit on wet grass, while he tried to kiss her. And if she said she hated it, he would make her sit in some awful tea-room while he talked more about sex.

But before she could answer, Mr Mybug continued, 'I thought we might do some walks together, if you'd care to? I'd better warn you – I'm – I have very few defences against—'

'Damp weather?' she said, pleasantly. 'Then perhaps we had better postpone our walks until the weather is finer. It would be sad if you could not make progress on your book because you caught a cold, and if you really have a weak chest, you cannot be too careful.'

Mr Mybug looked a little confused at this, but did not

somehow feel like explaining what he had really meant to Flora. He was not used to talking to young women who looked as clean and pure as she did.

Just then Flora noticed through the teashop window that the street outside was full of the Brothers, streaming out into the darkness. She put on her gloves and rose to her feet.

'I must go, I am afraid. My cousin will be looking for me. Goodbye. It's been so interesting. Perhaps we shall meet again sometime . . .'

Mr Mybug jumped at this remark, which Flora had let slip unintentionally, and said eagerly, 'It would be great fun if we could meet again. Here is my card.' And he brought out a large, dirty, nasty one with his name and address on, which Flora rather unwillingly put into her bag.

'I warn you,' he added, 'I'm a strange, moody creature. Nobody likes me, but there's something in me if you care to dig for it.'

Flora did not care to dig, but she said goodbye again and hurried across the road to join Amos. He had seen Mr Mybug in the teashop, and was looking at Flora with a face as black as thunder.

'Wicked woman!' he cried, pointing at her.

'No, really, Cousin Amos, that wasn't a stranger. I met him at a party in London,' protested Flora. 'And we were only having coffee.'

''Tes all the same – aye, and worse, him comin' from London, the devil's city,' said Amos darkly.

But he did not take his accusation any further, and only pointed out that Flora had missed a good deal by not staying for the shaking. Flora replied that she was sure she had, but that his powerful preaching had been too much for her weak and sinful spirit. She also mentioned the Ford van to him again, and was pleased to see that he was actively considering her suggestion. They drove the rest of the way home in silence.

By the third week in March, Flora felt that most of her plans were going well, although she had not succeeded with Adam. She had bought him an attractive little mop to wash the dishes with, but when she gave it to him, he took it and stared dreamily at it, his eyes like sightless ocean pools. ''Tes mine,' he murmured. ''Tes mine. Aye – my own liddle mop!' He pushed it inside his shirt to keep it safe.

'Yes. It's to cletter the dishes with,' said Flora firmly.

'Nay, nay,' protested Adam. ''Tes too pretty to cletter those nasty old dishes wi'. I mun do that wi' th' stick I always use. I'll keep my liddle mop in the cowshed, wi' the dumb creatures.'

'They might eat it,' suggested Flora.

'Aye, so they might. Well, I mun hang it up above the sink. 'Tes prettier than a flower, my liddle mop.' He hung it carefully on the wall above the taps, and stood admiring it for some time. Flora was annoyed, and went crossly out for a walk.

She often received letters from her friends. Mary Smiling wrote frequently. Charles also wrote in reply to Flora's little notes, giving her details about the weather in his part of the country and messages from his mother. Whatever else he wrote about, Flora seemed to find it extremely satisfying, and she looked forward to his letters. So, although she was a long way from her friends, she was not lonely.

Occasionally, while taking her daily walk on the hills, she saw Elfine in the distance, and decided she must find out more about her. She had heard from Adam how much time Elfine and

Richard Hawk-Monitor spent together, and although it was a delicate matter, she asked Adam when the young couple were planning to marry.

The old man gave a short, unpleasant laugh. 'Nothin' like that!' he replied. 'She thinks she's in love wi' him, and he – he likes women too much. He'll take her, and ruin her – that's what'll happen.'

Flora felt that was unlikely. Probably, Richard Hawk-Monitor was only slightly attracted by Elfine, and would never think of behaving as Adam feared. But it was even less likely that he would want to marry her. Young country gentlemen generally spent their time hunting, fishing and shooting. They liked their dogs well trained and their girls well dressed. They hated fuss, and talkative people, and they were always bored by poetry (Flora was sure Elfine wrote poems).

'So, unless I do something about it,' thought Flora, 'Richard simply won't think of proposing to her. And *no one* will want to marry her while she looks like that and wears those dresses. Except Mr Mybug, of course.'

But at the moment Mr Mybug was in love with Flora herself, so that was another problem. And was it quite fair to throw Elfine, all unprepared, into London's intellectual circles? No, Elfine must be civilized, and then she must marry Richard.

So Flora continued to look for Elfine when she went out for walks on the hills.

***

Meanwhile, Aunt Ada Doom sat in her room upstairs, alone. She was the centre of the house, the centre of the family, and she was, like all centres, completely alone.

I will not see my niece . . . Keep her away . . . Make some

51

excuse. Shut her out. She has been here a month and I have not seen her. I do not want to see her. But I can feel the warm wind of the approaching spring . . . Rubbing the walls of my house like sleepy cows . . . I am sleepy myself . . . The spring is coming . . .

When I was very small, I saw something nasty in the woodshed. I have never forgotten it. I never spoke of it to Mother, but I have remembered it all my life.

That was what has made me . . . different. What I saw in the toolshed made my life seem like a bad dream. Even now that I am seventy-nine, I cannot see a bicycle go past my bedroom window without having a sick feeling in my stomach . . . It was in the bicycle shed I saw it, something nasty, when I was very small.

That was why I stayed in this room. I've been here for twenty years, ever since Judith married and her husband came to live at the farm. I ran away from the huge, terrifying world outside these four walls, against which my thoughts rub themselves like sleepy lions. Yes, that's what they are like. Lions. Exactly like lions.

Outside in the world there are garden sheds where nasty things can happen. But nothing can happen here. And I will not allow any of the family to leave the farm, and go out into the great dirty world where nasty things happen in cowsheds. I hold all my family in my hand. None of them has any money, except what I give them. I allow tenpence each week to Micah, Urk, Caraway, Mark, Luke, and Ezra. Harkaway gets a shilling, to cover his bus fare to Beershorn and back when he pays the farm's profits into the bank every Saturday. Seth, my darling, my favourite grandchild, has one shilling and sixpence. Amos gets nothing. Judith gets nothing.

So here I sit, living from meal to meal. Day slips into day, season into season, year into year. And I sit here, alone. I am Cold Comfort Farm.

Sometimes Urk comes to see me, and tells me the farm is failing, falling into ruin, losing money.

No matter. There have always been Starkadders at Cold Comfort Farm.

Well, let it fail ... Nobody can have a farm without sheds (for wood, tools, bicycles, cows, the garden), and where there are sheds, things are bound to fall into ruin ... Besides, from what I can see from the farm accounts (which I check twice a week), things aren't doing too badly ... Anyway, here I am, and here they all are with me.

I've told them I am mad. I've been mad ever since I saw something nasty in the woodshed, years ago. If any of them went away, to any other part of the country, I'd go much madder. In fact, any attempt by any of them to get away from the farm always makes one of my attacks of madness come on. It's unfortunate in some ways but useful in others ... The woodshed experience damaged something in my child-brain all those years ago.

And it's because of that experience so many years ago that I sit up here, controlling everything and everyone, and having five meals a day brought up to me, so I suppose it wasn't such bad luck, seeing something nasty in the woodshed that day.

6

Help for Reuben and Elfine

The bull was bellowing. Seth leaned moodily on the gate, watching Reuben repair part of the fence. The air smelled of spring, and a bird sang foolishly from the cowshed roof.

Both brothers looked up as Flora came across the yard for her morning walk. She looked enquiringly at the shed where Big Business was still bellowing noisily.

'I think it would be a good idea if you let him out,' she said. Seth smiled wickedly, and Reuben's face went a dull red.

'I don't mean, with the cows,' Flora added. 'I meant simply for air and exercise. He shouldn't be shut up in the smelly dark all day.'

Seth disapproved of the impersonal note the conversation had taken, and walked away. But Reuben was always ready to listen to advice about improvements to the farm, and he said, quite pleasantly, 'Aye, 'tes true. We mun let him out in the great field tomorrow.' Just as Flora was walking away, he added, 'So ye went wi' the old devil, did ye?'

Flora was learning how to translate the Starkadder language, and understood 'the old devil' to refer to Amos. She replied, with a touch of polite surprise, 'I am not quite sure what you mean, but if you mean did I go with Cousin Amos to the Beershorn meeting of the Shaking Brothers, yes, I did.'

'And did the old devil say anything about me?'

Flora could only remember a remark about stepping into dead men's shoes, which it would scarcely be wise to repeat, so she said, 'I am afraid the preaching was so powerful that I really cannot remember anything else that was said. I have advised Cousin Amos to preach to a wider audience. I think he should go round the country in a Ford van, preaching—'

'Frightening the harmless birds off the bushes, more like,' interrupted Reuben crossly.

'—on market days. You see, if Cousin Amos were away a good deal, someone else would have to take charge of the farm.'

'Someone else will have to take charge of it in any case when the old devil dies,' said Reuben. Passion made his eyes flash and his breath come in gasps.

'Yes, of course,' said Flora. 'Now, if he could be persuaded to go away on a long preaching tour round England, whoever is left in charge could reorganize things here, to make the farm run more smoothly and efficiently. Then, when Cousin Amos did come back at last, he would see that the management of the farm must be left in the hands of that person, who would obviously be the best person for the job.'

'And who is that person – you?' he asked angrily.

'No, indeed. I've already told you, Reuben, that I would be no use at all at running the farm. I wish you'd believe me.'

Reuben looked puzzled. 'If ye don't mean you, who do you mean?'

Flora abandoned the delicate approach and said, 'You.'

'Me?'

'Aye, you.' She patiently dropped into Starkadder language, in order to improve communication.

He stared thickly at her. ''Tes impossible,' he said at last. 'The old lady would never let him go.'

'Why not?' asked Flora. 'Why does Aunt Ada Doom like to keep you all here, as though you were all children?'

'She's – she's ill,' said Reuben uneasily, glancing up at the closed, dusty windows above his head. 'If any of us leaves, or says we'll leave, she has an attack.'

'An attack? What of?' Flora was becoming a little impatient. Unlike Charles, she did not enjoy a mystery.

'Well, she's – she's mad.' Fat and dark, the word lay between them in the air.

'Oh,' said Flora thoughtfully. So that was it. Anyone might have expected a mad grandmother at Cold Comfort, and anyone would have been right. 'That's very awkward,' she observed.

'Aye, 'tes terrible. An' her madness takes the form of wantin' to know everything that goes on. She sees all the account books twice a week. An' if anyone does anything she doesn't like, she has an attack. 'Tes terrible.'

'It is indeed,' agreed Flora. It seemed to her that Aunt Ada Doom's madness had taken the most convenient form possible. 'Well, anyway, just because Aunt Ada is mad, there's no reason why you shouldn't try to persuade Cousin Amos to go on a preaching tour. Then you can manage the farm while he is away. Do try.'

Reuben's face took on a number of different expressions as he considered this, and suddenly, as she watched, victory was hers! 'Aye,' he said, 'I'll do it!' And much to her surprise, he held out his hand to her. She took it and shook it warmly. This was the first sign of human feeling she had met among the Starkadders, and she was moved by it.

It was a fresh, pleasant morning as she started her walk. She knew she would enjoy it more because Mr Mybug was not with her. For the last three mornings he had accompanied her, but this morning she had suggested he ought to do some writing. It cannot be said that Flora really enjoyed taking her walks with Mr Mybug. The problem was that he was not really interested in anything except sex. This was understandable, if unfortunate. After all, many of our best minds have had the same weakness. But it meant that everything Mr Mybug saw reminded him of sex – the hills, the trees, the flowers. He pointed them all out, and asked Flora what she thought. She found it difficult to reply, because she was not interested. He then remarked how strange it was that young Englishwomen were so cold. How important it was to be free and natural! Just to throw off your clothes if you felt like it! To give way to your desires! So delicious! So simple! So *real*!

So, on the whole, Flora was pleased to have her walk alone.

Just then, as she came round the side of a hill, she saw Elfine sitting on the grass in the sun. Both cousins were surprised, but Flora was quite pleased. She wanted a chance to talk to Elfine.

Elfine jumped to her feet, and stood staring at Flora.

'You're Flora – I'm Elfine,' she said simply.

'No prizes offered,' thought Flora, rather rudely. Aloud, she said politely, 'Yes. Isn't it a lovely morning? Have you been far?'

'Yes . . . No . . . Away over there . . .' A wild movement of her arm showed no limit to her wanderings. Judith made similarly sweeping movements; there was not a vase left anywhere in the farmhouse.

'Do you like poetry?' Elfine asked suddenly. 'I love it. It says all the things I can't say for myself . . . somehow . . . It means . . . oh, I don't know. Just everything, somehow. It's *enough*. Do you ever feel that?'

'Occasionally,' replied Flora cautiously.

'I write poetry,' said Elfine. (So I was right! thought Flora.) 'I'll show you some . . . if you promise not to laugh. I call my poems my children. And love, too,' she added in a lower voice, 'love and poetry go together, somehow, don't they?'

Flora said sternly, 'Elfine, are you engaged?'

Her cousin stood still, the colour leaving her face. She bent her head. 'There's someone . . . We don't want to spoil things by making any definite arrangement . . . It's horrible . . . to take away anyone's freedom.'

'Nonsense,' said Flora. 'It is a very good idea. Now, what do you suppose will happen to you if you don't marry this Someone?'

Elfine looked more cheerful. 'Oh, I've got it all planned. I'll go and get a job in a shop, somewhere by the sea, and in my spare time I'll do some painting, and make things . . .'

'And that would be *most* unsuitable,' said Flora coldly. But she felt sorry when she noticed how miserable Elfine was looking, and went on to say, in a very friendly way, 'Now what is the matter? Tell me.'

'It's . . . it's Urk,' whispered Elfine. 'He . . . they . . . I think he wants to marry me, and Grandmother intends us to marry when I am eighteen. He sometimes climbs up the apple-tree outside my window and watches me undressing . . . I have to hang a towel over the window. I don't know what to do.'

Flora was extremely angry, but did not show it. It was at this moment that she decided to adopt Elfine and rescue her from all the Starkadders.

'And does this Someone know about Urk?'

'Well . . . I told him, and he just said, "Bad luck, old girl".'

'It's Dick Hawk-Monitor, isn't it? Forgive my asking you these questions, Elfine, but does he seem to love you?'

'He . . . he does when I'm there, Flora, but I don't somehow think he thinks much about me when I'm not there. Perhaps I'm selfish, but I *would* like us to get married. You know, Flora, there's a dangerous cousin called Pamela, who often comes down from London for weekends. Dick thinks she's great fun.'

Flora felt depressed when she heard this. It would be difficult enough to win Dick for Elfine anyway; it would be a thousand times more difficult against a rival.

'. . . And then there's his birthday dance,' Elfine was saying. 'I did rather want to go, because it's Dick's twenty-first, and it's going to be a proper ball, but of course Grandmother would not allow me to go. She doesn't allow Starkadders to accept any invitations, except to funerals, and she thinks dancing is wicked. Dick did say he wished I was going, but perhaps he was only being kind.'

'Now, listen, Elfine, I think it would be an excellent plan if you went to this ball. I shall go, too, to keep an eye on you. I will ask one of my friends to try to get some invitations for us. And then I will take you up to London with me, to have your hair done and buy you an evening dress.'

'Oh, Flora!' Flora was pleased to see that Elfine's wild-bird look was beginning to disappear, and that she was talking quite naturally. A well-cut dress and a fashionable hairstyle might make her look really lovely.

'I will ask a friend of mine, Claud Hart-Harris, to write to Mrs Hawk-Monitor,' said Flora. 'I expect he knows her – he knows so many people! He can be my partner.' (She had decided not to ask Charles, as she felt she needed to keep a clear head for this occasion, and might take too personal an interest in the success of the evening if he were there.) 'But *you* must have a partner too, you know. Does Seth dance?'

'I don't know. I hate him,' replied Elfine, simply.

'I cannot say I like him that much myself,' confessed Flora, 'but I do not think there is anyone else we can ask.' Of course Mr Mybug would be available, she thought. It was dreadful having no choice except Seth or Mr Mybug, but Sussex was like that.

That day Flora wrote to Claud Hart-Harris, who replied with admirable speed and efficiency. He knew Dick's mother, who was a charming woman. He could certainly arrange four invitations, and would be delighted to go as Flora's partner. Flora began to feel a little ashamed of her plan. The 'charming woman' might not consider Elfine the ideal wife for her son. Elfine would have to change completely, inside and out, before Mrs Hawk-Monitor could consider her suitable. And even then, Dick's mother could not possibly approve of Elfine's family. And the Starkadders themselves would no doubt be extremely angry when the engagement was announced.

Difficult times lay ahead. But this is what Flora liked, fighting battles in a cool and organized way. She decided to start training Elfine immediately. There would be no more poetry, or long walks, unless Elfine were accompanied by the proper sort of dog to take on long walks. She must learn to be serious about horses. She must learn to laugh when music or books were mentioned, and to confess that she was not brainy. She must learn to be polite, and dress carefully, and brush her hair. And there was such a very short time to teach her these things!

A few days later, when Flora had gone into Beershorn by bus to do some shopping, she met one of the Starkadders, Harkaway. He was performing his weekly task of paying the farm's profits into the bank, and had driven into Beershorn in the horse and trap (in this way he saved the shilling his grandmother gave him every week for the bus fare). He stared suspiciously at Flora, but offered to drive her back to the farm. She accepted, as she was always glad to see more of the private lives of the Starkadders.

She began to make polite conversation. 'How are you all getting on with the new well you're building?'

''Tes all fallen down. 'Tes terrible.'

'Oh, I am so sorry! What a pity! How did it happen?'

'Mark an' Micah were arguing an' Mark pushed Micah down th' well. Laugh! We had to lie down, we were laughin' so much.'

'Was – is Micah – er – is he badly hurt?'

'Nay. But th' bricks are all broken. Th' old lady won't be pleased when she finds out.'

'Ah, yes, my aunt,' said Flora thoughtfully. 'I cannot understand why you do not break away from her.'

'She's mad. If any of us left th' farm, she'd go madder still. That would be a terrible thing. We mun keep the head o' the family alive an' in good health. There have always been—'

'I know, I know,' interrupted Flora. 'So comforting, isn't it? But really, Harkaway, I do think it is strange when grown men are prevented from marrying—'

Harkaway laughed shortly, and said, 'Nay, nay. Most of us are married. But th' old lady, she mun never see our wives. So our women live down i' th' village. Micah, Mark, Luke, Caraway, and Ezra have all got wives. Me . . . I've got my own troubles.'

Flora wanted to ask what his own troubles were, but feared that this might produce a flood of embarrassing secrets. Perhaps he was in love with Mrs Beetle? Meanwhile, his news was so surprising that she could only stare and stare again. 'Do you mean to say there are five Starkadder wives living in the village?'

'Aye, five, and Rennet, o' course. Poor Rennet . . .'

'Who's Rennet, and what is the matter with *her*?' asked Flora, rather sharply. She was upset to hear there were so many more Starkadders to deal with.

'She's Micah's wife's daughter, from when Micah's wife was married to Mark. She's never married. She's a bit strange i' th' head. Sometimes when the sukebind hangs heavy from the branches, she jumps down th' old well. 'Tes Nature, ye might say, turned sour in her blood.'

Flora wanted to hear no more. She felt she could not possibly rescue these women as well as Elfine. They would just have to manage for themselves.

For the next three weeks she was so busy with Elfine that she had no time to worry about the unknown female Starkadders. She was delighted to find out that Elfine was more than ready to give up her strangeness of dress, attitude, and behaviour, if something better was shown to her. Also, she was only seventeen, and underneath the poetry and painting and dreams, Flora found her to be a friendly and sweet-tempered girl, capable of loving calmly and deeply, and fond of pretty things. As the weeks passed, Elfine grew more confident and happier with her new self, and looked forward to sharing Richard Hawk-Monitor's life. Flora knew what a disaster it would be for Elfine if the plan did not succeed.

On April 19th Flora came down to breakfast with a pleasant feeling of excitement. She was looking out for the postman, because today was the day the invitations were supposed to arrive from Hightree Hall. It was a relief to see that none of the Starkadders seemed to be around. She did not want any of them to see the letter and perhaps interfere with her plans.

Just then the bull bellowed loudly. Flora looked thoughtfully out at his shed. She spoke to Mrs Beetle, who was cleaning the kitchen. 'Mrs Beetle, the bull ought to be let out. Can you help me? Are you afraid of bulls?'

'Yes,' said Mrs Beetle. 'I *am* afraid of bulls. I'll go up to your bedroom window, miss, and shout at him from there.' She rushed away before Flora could stop her, and a few seconds later, she shouted down from Flora's window, 'Go on, miss, I'm here!'

Flora was now rather frightened. The situation seemed to have developed much faster than she had expected. Big Business bellowed again, a sound full of sorrow and suffering. Flora ran across the yard and pushed open the gate leading to the big field. She went back to the bull's shed, and opened the door.

Out came Big Business. He stood for a second or two, confused by the light, his big head moving stupidly from side to side.

'Go on, ye old horror!' shouted Mrs Beetle.

Slowly the bull moved his huge body across the yard and into the field. Flora followed cautiously, and banged the gate shut behind him. She went back into the kitchen for her breakfast.

But unfortunately, just as she was drinking her tea, she noticed the postman and another figure in conversation, some distance from the house. And soon Urk Starkadder entered the kitchen. He had been out shooting that morning, and a number

63

of small dead animals hung round his neck and from his belt. Flora saw that he was holding several envelopes, and that his bloodstained thumb had made a red mark on an envelope addressed to her in Charles's neat handwriting. She was extremely annoyed. 'My letters, please,' she said firmly, holding out her hand.

Urk gave her the one from Charles, but he kept the second, turning it over to look at the address on the back. 'It's from th' Hawk-Monitors at Hightree Hall,' he said in an evil, low, throaty voice. 'Ye're clever, aren't ye? Ye think I don't know what's goin' on? Well, just listen to me. Elfine's mine, I tell you . . . mine. She was promised to me the day she was born, by her grandmother. I put a cross in water-vole's blood on her milk-bottle, when she was an hour old, to show she's mine. An' this summer, when the water-voles play in the stream, I'll make her mine!' And he turned and walked out of the kitchen.

'Well!' said Mrs Beetle. 'What a nasty temper!'

Flora made up her mind to waste no time. She would take Elfine up to London that very day, instead of tomorrow, as she had planned. If Urk suspected that they were going to the ball, he would probably try to stop them. Whatever happened, they must get Elfine's dress. She hurried away, to ask Seth to drive them to the station to catch the 10.59 train. He was only too willing, as he was looking forward to going to the ball and comparing it with ones he had seen in films. And in a few minutes, the trap was in the yard, with Seth holding the horse.

Just then, old Adam appeared at the door of the cowshed. 'Someone's let the bull out!' he cried. ''Tes terrible! Who let 'un out?'

'I did,' said Flora, coming out into the yard with Elfine.

Distant shouts came from the back of the farm, from Micah and Ezra.

'The bull's out! Who let 'un out?'

'Who let Big Business out? 'Tes terrible!'

Flora had been writing on a page from her notebook, which she now gave to Adam, telling him to attach it to the kitchen door. It said: *I did. F. Poste.*

'The bull's out! Who let 'un out?'

'Who let th' bull out?' shouted Reuben, appearing from a field. Flora pointed silently to the note.

'Who let th' bull out?' screamed Judith, from an upstairs window. And Amos repeated the question as he came running into the yard.

But Flora, Elfine and Seth were off. The horse and trap moved away from the farm. Flora just stopped herself bowing from side to side, or giving a royal wave, as they passed through the gate.

7

The Hawk-Monitor ball

They passed a pleasant day in London. Flora first took Elfine to her favourite hairdresser, who cut Elfine's hair short and brushed it into a careless, simple, extremely expensive style. Then they went to her dressmaker, a world-famous Frenchman who made all Flora's clothes for her. His eyes widened when he saw Elfine. He looked at her wide shoulders and long legs, and reached blindly towards a roll of snow-coloured silk that a well-trained assistant put into his arms.

'White?' suggested Flora cautiously.

'But what else?' screamed the Frenchman, seizing his scissors to cut the silk. 'It is to wear white that God, once in a hundred years, makes a young girl like this.'

Flora watched for an hour while he cut and tore and folded the silk. She was pleased to see that Elfine did not seem nervous or bored, but enjoyed being the centre of attention.

At one o'clock one of Flora's friends, Julia, came to take them to lunch at the New River Club.

'Well, do you like your new dress?' Flora asked Elfine.

'It's heavenly,' said Elfine seriously. 'It's better than poetry, Flora.' Flora was pleased. She was spending a lot of money on

Elfine, but she did not mind, if it meant defeating the Starkadders.

That afternoon Flora took the opportunity of attending a concert, one of the civilized pleasures she had been missing lately, while Julia took Elfine shopping for underwear, shoes, and an evening coat. In the evening they all went to an amusing play at a theatre, and then Flora and Elfine spent the night at a quiet, respectable hotel.

The next morning they collected the finished dress, and when they arrived back at Beershorn station, Flora was pleasantly surprised to see Seth waiting to meet them with the horse and trap. On the way to the farm, they stopped at a large garage, to arrange for a car to collect Claud Hart-Harris from the station the following day, and then come to pick them up from Cold Comfort, before taking all four of them to the Hawk-Monitor ball.

'Are you looking forward to it, Seth?' Flora asked cheerfully, as they drove up to the farm.

'Aye,' he answered softly, in his warm voice. ''Twill be the first time I've ever been to a dance where all the women aren't chasing me. Girls are all th' same. They mun have every bit of your time and your thoughts. But I'm not like that. I only like films.'

Seth's problem was the next on her list, thought Flora. She had a letter in her handbag from an American friend of hers, Earl P. Neck, who was coming to see her in Sussex in the next few days. Mr Neck was a film producer in Hollywood, and Flora was going to introduce Seth to him.

At five o'clock on the evening of the next day, the cousins were beginning to get ready. It was a mild, rosy spring evening, with birds singing in the trees and the air smelling of leaves and freshness.

The intelligent and sensitive reader will no doubt have wondered during this story what the bathroom arrangements were at Cold Comfort. The answer is simple. There was no bathroom. The Starkadders managed without that modern convenience. However, Flora had discovered that capable Mrs Beetle had a tin bath, which she allowed Flora to use every other evening, for a small weekly payment.

But tonight, just when baths were needed, baths were impossible. So Flora heated a large quantity of water on the kitchen fire, and took it up to her bedroom, where Elfine was waiting. Fortunately, the Starkadders did not seem to have noticed the girls' absence from the farm the previous night. But Aunt Ada – did she know? If she found out they were going to the dance, she would certainly stop them.

'She may come downstairs one of these evenings,' said Elfine fearfully. 'She sometimes does, in the spring.'

'I hope she enjoys it,' said Flora, almost rudely.

'And the sukebind is ready to flower,' added Elfine.

'That dark green plant?' said Flora. 'I suppose when its flowers open, the trouble begins, does it?' But there was no time for more conversation; the serious business of dressing had to begin.

Perhaps something in the restless air of the spring evening had entered the room where old Aunt Ada sat in front of her dying fire. She suddenly rang a small bell, which brought Judith to her side.

'I mun go downstairs,' said the old woman.

'Mother, you're mistaken. 'Tes not the first o' May nor th' seventeenth of October. You'd better stay here.'

'I tell you I mun go downstairs. I mun feel you all around me. Help me with my clothes, girl.'

Silently, Judith obeyed. The old house was silent, and Aunt Ada's thoughts turned in circles.

Once . . . when I was a little girl . . . I saw something nasty in the woodshed. Now I am old . . . but I remember . . .

In her bedroom, Flora was standing back, looking at Elfine with great satisfaction.

'Oh, Flora . . . do I look nice?'

'You look extremely beautiful,' replied Flora. 'Make sure you behave properly.' She felt that her own appearance, in a pale green dress and blue-green evening coat, was modestly pleasing.

They had a whole hour to wait before the car arrived. To calm them, Flora read aloud from *The Thoughts of Father Bertrand*. She did hope that everything would go as planned. So much could go wrong! Above all, would Richard Hawk-Monitor propose marriage to Elfine? Even Flora did not dare imagine what would happen if they returned from the ball and he had not asked her. He *must* propose! She prayed to the god of love, by the spring evening, by the song of the birds, by the amazing beauty of Elfine, to make it happen.

There was a knock on the door. It was Seth, informing them in a whisper that a car was approaching.

'Is Urk anywhere near?' asked Flora, slightly nervously.

'I saw him hanging over th' well, talking to th' water-voles an hour ago,' replied Seth.

'Oh, then, I think we can go down without fear of seeing him,' said Flora. 'Are you ready, Elfine? Come along.'

By the light of Seth's candle they made their way to the empty kitchen. Outside in the yard they saw a large car, with driver, waiting for them. Flora saw to her relief that Claud was looking out of the car window. She waved to him, just catching the words '*too* primitive' floating across the still evening air.

'I'll carry Elfine. She mun never spoil her shoes,' whispered Seth, with unexpected thoughtfulness, and picking up his sister, he carried her across the dirty yard. He made a second journey for Flora, and soon they were all four inside the car. Seth gave instructions to the driver, who nodded and started the car.

'My dear Flora, you look extremely nice,' said Claud, taking her hands. 'Now tell me all about it.' And Flora told him the whole story in a low voice. He was both amused and interested. Claud had fought for his country in the recent war and seen his friends die in terrible pain, so for him the whole of the rest of his life was an entertaining game which no man of taste and intelligence could permit himself to take seriously.

The ball was being held in Godmere, a town near Beershorn, in the Grand Hotel there. Flora's driver stopped near the main entrance to the hotel, to let his passengers get out. Flora instructed him to return to pick them up at midnight.

There was a red carpet leading up the steps to the impressive double doors of the building. All around was an admiring crowd, come to enjoy the sight of so many well-born, wealthy and elegant people. Just as Flora was going up the steps, she thought she heard someone say her name, and when she turned her head, she realized it was Mr Mybug. He had climbed halfway up a lamp-post in order to get a better view of the guests. He waved cheerfully enough at her, but she felt a little sorry for him, because he was rather fat and his clothes were not very good, and when she compared him with Charles, she considered him a rather sad figure.

'Who is that?' inquired Claud, glancing in that direction.

'A Mr Mybug. I met him in London.'

'How awful!' observed Claud, deeply disgusted.

Flora felt she could not risk speaking to Mr Mybug, as she was there as Elfine's chaperone, and must make sure her own behaviour was absolutely faultless. So she just bowed pleasantly to him, and her party continued up the steps and into the hotel.

Not only were there steps leading up to the front doors, but also wide, curving stairs inside, which led down into the large ballroom. When Flora saw these beautiful stairs, she was so grateful to the god of love that she could have knelt down and thanked him. Did Father Bertrand not say in his *Thoughts*, 'Lost is that man who sees a beautiful woman descending a grand staircase', and did Flora not have both these things here? What else but a staircase could so perfectly show the jewel she had made of Elfine?

A handsome lady of about sixty stood at the top of the stairs to welcome her guests. The four young people from Cold Comfort slowly approached their hostess. Flora noticed what a good moment it was for their arrival. It was nearly nine o'clock, and all the guests of importance had already arrived. The finest young men and women in Sussex were dancing in the ballroom below, as Claud moved forward to introduce Flora, Elfine, and Seth to Mrs Hawk-Monitor. Then Elfine, gently urged forward by Flora, began to descend the red-carpeted stairs.

It was at this moment that the music stopped and the dance ended, and the dancers below stood still, clapping and smiling. A sudden silence fell, as all eyes turned towards the stairs. A low murmur of admiration, the most delightful sound in the world to a woman's ears, rose into the stillness.

*'Lost is that man who sees a beautiful woman
descending a grand staircase.'*

Here was beauty, simple and pure. It silenced all comment
except that of eager praise. Just as no human being can deny the
beauty of a rose in full flower, no human eyes could deny Elfine's
beauty. And Flora, silently watching, saw that a tall young man

at the bottom of the stairs was looking up at Elfine as though she were a goddess; and she was satisfied.

The music began again, and the young man (Richard Hawk-Monitor himself) came forward to give his hand to Elfine and lead her into the dance. Flora and Claud also joined the dancers.

Flora had every reason to feel satisfied with her evening's work as she floated round the room in the arms of Claud, who danced admirably. She could see, as she observed Elfine and her partner, that Richard appeared to be deeply in love. The love god had answered Flora's prayer, and Richard had realized, not that Elfine was beautiful, but that he loved her. (Flora knew that it is frequently necessary to point out this fact to young men.) Now Flora had to wait patiently till the end of the ball, when Elfine would tell her whether Richard had proposed marriage or not.

However, she began to enjoy the ball so much that she almost forgot her anxiety about her cousin's future. It was indeed a very pleasant ball, as there were a large number of guests, most of whom knew each other slightly. The richness of the furnishings and the elegance of the supper added to the success of the evening.

Elfine danced most of the dances with Richard, but she also danced with some of the eager young men who gathered round her as soon as the music stopped. Flora noticed that Mrs Hawk-Monitor was beginning to look anxious, especially when Elfine was dancing with Richard. Flora herself divided her dances between Claud and Seth. Several young men approached her and asked her to dance, which pleased her, but she had decided that she would not be a rival to Elfine that evening. She knew she did not look as beautiful as Elfine, but considered that she looked distinguished, elegant, and interesting, and asked for nothing more. Seth was also enjoying himself, with a crowd of London beauties, and was almost as much admired as Elfine.

Flora and Claud sat for a long time over their supper, enjoying the sight of a crowd of happy young people laughing and talking. As at all good parties, an atmosphere, untouchable as a perfume but as real, rose above the heads of the smiling guests. There was an air of enjoyment and cheerfulness, which was breathed by everyone, an invisible cloud of success over the whole evening.

Suddenly Flora realized Elfine had appeared at the door of the supper-room, accompanied by Richard. They were glancing round as if in search of someone, and when Flora lifted her hand in its pale green glove, Elfine smiled eagerly and hurried towards her. She arrived at their table, hand in hand with Richard, and said breathlessly, 'Oh, Flora, I do so want you to meet Dick.'

Flora bowed and smiled, and said, 'How do you do? I have heard so much about you.'

'I say, I'm awfully glad to meet you, Miss Poste. Elfine has told me all about you, too. I simply can't thank you enough for bringing Elfine. We're engaged, as a matter of fact.'

'My dear! How charming! I am delighted! I congratulate you!' cried Flora, who was indeed overcome with relief and satisfaction.

'Charming,' murmured Claud, behind her.

'We're going to announce it at the end of the ball,' said Richard. 'Good opportunity, don't you think?'

Claud, wondering how Dick's mother would feel when she heard the news, agreed it was the ideal moment. Conversation continued among the four young people, until the music started again for the final dance.

As Flora danced with Claud, she observed how happy and

75

beautiful Elfine looked in Richard's arms. 'I have achieved my aim,' she thought contentedly. 'Elfine is rescued. From now on her life will be normal. She will have children, and they will be pleasant, ordinary English people who have poetry in their secret souls. That is as it should be.'

In the pause that followed the music, Flora noticed that Richard was leading Elfine up the stairs, to where his mother was sitting with some old friends. After a few words to his mother, Richard turned to the guests below, and held up his hand for silence.

'Ladies and gentlemen, it's been awfully good seeing you all here tonight,' he said. 'I'll always be glad to remember you were all here on my twenty-first birthday. Good fun, isn't it?' There was laughter and some clapping. Flora held her breath. He must – he *must* announce the engagement now!

But it was all right. He was speaking again, pulling Elfine gently forward towards the guests. 'And this is a particularly wonderful evening for me, because I've got something else to tell you all. I want to tell you that Miss Starkadder and I are engaged.' There! It was out! There was a storm of clapping and excited comment, and people began streaming up the stairs to offer their congratulations. Flora felt quite weak after the nervous excitement of the past five minutes, but, as Elfine's chaperone, made herself go to say a few words to Dick's mother.

Mrs Hawk-Monitor was, naturally, extremely shocked at the suddenness of the engagement, but Flora was able to persuade her that she would soon grow to love Elfine for her sweetness and honesty. Flora took the opportunity to advise a short engagement and an early wedding, to avoid any unpleasantness with the Starkadders.

Finally Flora and her party said goodbye to the Hawk-Monitors and got into their car. They left Claud at Beershorn station, and started the long drive back to Cold Comfort. Flora was rather tired after such a busy few days, and slept for a while in the car. She woke to hear Seth and Elfine arguing.

'Aye, th' old lady'll have something to say about what happened tonight.'

'Grandmother can't stop me getting married!'

'She'll certainly try. You wait an' see.'

'I think Elfine will marry very soon,' interrupted Flora coldly, 'so she must avoid Aunt Ada while she's in the house. That won't be very difficult, as Aunt Ada never leaves her bedroom.'

Seth gave a low, unpleasant laugh. They were just driving into the farmyard, and, leaning past Flora, Seth pointed through the car window at the farmhouse.

Flora stared in the direction in which he pointed and saw, to her horror, that instead of the usual total darkness, all the windows were brightly lit.

8

The Counting

'It's Grandmother!' whispered Elfine, who had gone very white. 'She must have chosen this night, of all nights, to come downstairs and have the family party.'

'Nonsense! You don't have parties at places like Cold Comfort,' said Flora, taking notes from her bag with which to pay the driver. She got out of the car, breathing in the fresh, sweet night air, and put them into his hand. 'There. Thank you very much. Good night.'

And the driver, having thanked her respectfully, drove out of the farmyard and away down the road. The friendly sound of the engine began to fade away, until it disappeared completely in the quiet of the night.

They all turned and looked towards the house. The lights in the windows looked unpleasantly like the faces of evil old men. A thin wind blew across the dark, muddy yard.

'Aye, 'tes Grandmother,' said Seth. 'She's holding the Counting. Aye, 'tes her, all right.'

'So what is the Counting, for heaven's sake,' said Flora crossly, beginning to pick her way across the yard, 'and why is it held at half-past one in the morning?'

'Ye see, we're violent people, we Starkadders. Some of us push others down wells. Some of us die o' drink or go mad. There's a whole crowd of us too. 'Tes difficult to keep count of us. So once a year Grandmother holds a gatherin', called the Counting, and she counts us all, to see how many of us have died i' th' year.'

'Well, she won't be counting *me*,' said Flora. 'Now, Elfine, this may be difficult. You had better not say a word. *I* will do the talking.'

And she knocked at the back door. For a few moments there was a silence they could almost touch. It was broken by heavy footsteps, and then the door was slowly opened. Urk stood looking at them, with an expression on his face that was a mixture of desire, anger, and misery.

The great kitchen was full of people. They were all silent, and all painted a hellish red by the firelight. Flora could distinguish most of the Starkadders. They were standing in a circle around someone who was sitting in a large high-backed chair by the fire. On the walls were hanging great bunches of sukebind, whose pink flowers had opened, filling the air with a powerful, sweet-smelling perfume. Everyone was staring at the door, completely still, like wax figures.

'Well, well,' said Flora pleasantly, stepping in and taking off her gloves. 'The gang *is* all here, isn't it? Is that Big Business in the corner? Oh, I'm sorry, it's Micah. I suppose there aren't any sandwiches?'

This cracked the social ice a bit. Signs of life were observed.

'There's food on th' table,' said Judith lifelessly, her burning eyes fixed upon Seth, 'but first, Robert Poste's child, ye must greet your Aunt Ada Doom.'

And she took Flora's hand (Flora was glad she had taken off

79

her clean glove) and led her up to the figure in the high-backed chair.

'How do you do, Aunt Ada?' said Flora, putting out her hand. But Aunt Ada made no effort to take it. She folded her own hands a little more closely upon a copy of the *Milk Producers' Weekly Magazine*, and observed, in a low expressionless voice, 'I saw something nasty in the woodshed.'

''Tes one of her bad nights,' said Judith. 'Mother,' she said more loudly, 'don't you know me? It's Judith. I have brought Robert Poste's child to see you.'

'Nay . . . I saw something nasty in the woodshed,' said Aunt Ada Doom, moving her old head from side to side. ''Twas sixty-nine years ago. An' me no bigger than a bird—'

Flora had been observing Aunt Ada's firm chin, clear eyes and tight little mouth, and decided that if Aunt Ada was mad, then she, Flora, was one of the Marx brothers.

'Saw something nasty in the woodshed!!!' suddenly screamed Aunt Ada, hitting Judith with the *Milk Producers' Weekly*. 'You're all wicked and cruel. You want to go away and leave me alone in the woodshed. But you never shall. None of you. Never! There have always been Starkadders at Cold Comfort. You must all stay here with me, Judith, Amos, Micah, Urk, Luke, Mark, Elfine, Caraway, Harkaway, Reuben, and Seth. Where's my darling Seth?'

Seth came pushing his way through the crowd of relations. 'Here I am, grandmother,' he said comfortingly. 'I'll never leave 'ee, never.'

'That's my good boy,' the old woman murmured. 'But how grand you are tonight! What's all this?' And she pulled at Seth's evening clothes. 'Where have you been, boy?'

Flora could see that there was no point in hiding the truth any longer, so she took a deep breath and said loudly and clearly, 'He's been to Godmere, to Richard Hawk-Monitor's twenty-first birthday dance. So have I. So has Elfine. So has a friend of mine called Claud, whom none of you know. And what is more, Aunt Ada, Elfine and Richard Hawk-Monitor are engaged to be married, and *will* be married, too, in about a month from now.'

There came a terrible cry from the shadows near the sink. Everybody turned to look. It was Urk, lying face downward in the sandwiches, with one hand holding his heart in dreadful pain. Meriam laid her rough hand shyly upon his bowed head, but he shook her off.

'My little water-vole,' they heard him murmur.

Confusion and shouting broke out, in which Aunt Ada could be seen beating at everybody with the *Milk Producers' Weekly,* while screaming, 'I shall go mad! There have always been Starkadders at Cold Comfort! I saw something nasty in the woodshed . . . something nasty . . . nasty . . .' Seth was holding her hands and speaking quietly to her, as to a sick child. Flora had pulled Elfine into a corner, out of the way, and was feeding both of them on bread and butter. She had given up all hope of going to bed that night. It was nearly half-past two, and everybody seemed happy to go on till sunrise.

She observed several females moving miserably around in the dark room, putting bread on plates and occasionally crying in corners.

'Who's that?' she asked Elfine, pointing at one who was crying half inside a boot cupboard.

''Tes poor Rennet,' said Elfine sleepily. 'You see her wet clothes? She jumped down th' well this evening, Meriam told me.

Grandmother was saying nasty things about Rennet not being able to find a man, and never gettin' married. So Rennet ran out an' jumped down th' well. And Grandmother had one of her attacks.'

'I'm not surprised,' murmured Flora, yawning. 'Oh, what's happening now?'

The noise coming from the crowd surrounding Aunt Ada had increased. By standing on a table, Flora and Elfine could distinguish Amos, who was leaning over Aunt Ada Doom's chair, and shouting loudly at her.

'. . . So I mun go where th' Lord's work calls me and spread th' Lord's word abroad in strange places. Ah, 'tes terrible to have to go, but I mun do it. I mun go abroad in a Ford van, preaching all over th' countryside. Aye, I have heard my call, and I mun follow it.' He threw his arms open wide and stood there with the firelight playing on his face.

'No . . . No!' screamed Aunt Ada Doom furiously. 'You mun never go! There have always been Starkadders at Cold Comfort. I shall go mad! I saw something nasty in the woodshed . . . Ah . . . ah . . .'

She struggled to her feet, supported by Seth and Judith, and struck weakly at Amos with the *Milk Producers' Weekly* (which was looking a bit damaged by this time). He did not move, but kept staring at some distant, heavenly vision.

'I mun go . . .' he repeated, in a strange, soft voice. 'I hear th' Lord callin' me across th' scranletted fields where the liddle vegetables are clapping their hands in prayer, and besides, I have to catch the coach to London, so I've no time to lose. Aye, 'tes goodbye to you all. Mother, I've broken your chain at last, wi' th' help o' th' Lord's word. Where's my hat?'

'I saw something nasty in the woodshed!'

Reuben passed it silently to his father (he had had it ready for the last ten minutes). Aunt Ada turned her eyes, holes of pain in her grey face, on Amos, and watched him move with great, slow steps to the door. No one moved. Amos pushed open the door.

'Amos!' she cried from her heart. But he never turned. He stepped into the dark – and was gone.

Suddenly there was a wild cry from the corner in the shadows by the sink. Urk fell forward, pulling Meriam after him. Flora woke up Elfine, who had gone to sleep on her shoulder, and told her that more fun was just beginning. It was only a quarter past three.

Urk was laughing madly, noiselessly. Meriam pulled herself away from him, her face white with fear.

'Me an' th' water-voles, we've failed,' Urk whispered. 'We're beaten. We planned a home for her near the well. An' now she's given herself to *him*! When she was an hour old, I made a mark on her milk-bottle with water-vole's blood. She was mine, see? Mine! And I've lost her . . .'

He turned upon Meriam, who stared at him in terror. 'Come here – you. I'll take you instead. Aye, dirt as ye are, we'll sink into th' mud together. There have always been Starkadders at Cold Comfort, and now there'll be a Beetle too.'

'And not the first either, as you'd know if you'd ever cleaned the kitchen,' said Mrs Beetle sharply. Flora had not noticed her before; she had been busily cutting bread in a far corner of the kitchen. She now came forward and said nastily to Urk, 'Who are you to talk about dirt? A pity you don't spend less time with your old water-voles and a bit more with some soap and hot water.' She turned to her daughter. 'Don't you have him unless you feel like it, dear,' she advised. 'You're still young and he won't see forty again.'

'I don't mind,' said Meriam. 'I'll have 'un, if he wants me. I can always make 'un wash a bit, if I want to.'

Urk gave a wild laugh. His hands fell on her shoulders, and, pulling her to him, he kissed her firmly on her open mouth. Aunt Ada Doom, shaking with anger, struck at them with the *Milk Producers' Weekly*, but missed. She fell back in her chair, exhausted.

'Come, my beauty, my handful of dirt. I mun carry 'ee up to th' well an' show 'ee to the water-voles,' said Urk, his eyes bright with desire.

'What! At this time of night?' cried Mrs Beetle, deeply shocked.

Urk put one arm round Meriam's waist and tried to lift her, but she was too heavy for him. So he made her stand in the middle of the floor, and with a low, passionate cry, ran to her. 'Come, my beauty!' He caught her up in his arms and continued towards the door, all in one movement. Mark (who loved a bit of sport) held open the door, and Urk and his load rushed out into the night.

Silence fell. The door remained open, swinging in a slow, cold wind which had just started blowing. As though frozen, the group in the kitchen waited for the distant crash which would tell them that Urk had fallen down.

Quite soon it came, and Mark shut the door.

It was now four o'clock, and Elfine had gone to sleep again. So had all the farmworkers. Flora was desperately sleepy; she felt as though she were at some awful modern play that goes on for hours and hours.

Aunt Ada was sitting in her chair, her lips moving softly. She did not sound very happy. 'Two of them . . . gone. Elfine . . . Amos . . . and I'm alone in the woodshed now. Who took them away? I must know . . . That girl . . . Robert Poste's child.' Her old face looked evil in the dying light of the fire. Suddenly, with the *Milk Producers' Weekly*, she struck at Rennet, who was standing close, staring madly down at her, and Rennet ran back to her dark corner. It was half-past four.

Just then Flora felt cold air at her back. She looked round crossly, and found herself looking into the face of Reuben, who had opened a small hidden door in the wall, which led out into the yard. 'Come on,' he whispered soundlessly. ''Tes time ye were in bed.'

Amazed and grateful, Flora silently woke Elfine, and cautiously they crept through the door, which Reuben closed behind them. They stood outside in the yard, in a bitter wind, with the first cold light of morning creeping into the purple sky. The way to their beds lay clear before them – round the house and in at the front door, avoiding the kitchen and the rest of the Starkadders.

'Reuben,' said Flora, too sleepy to speak properly, but remembering to be polite, 'you are *wonderful*. Why did you help us?'

'Because you got th' old devil out o' th' way for me. Th' farm will be mine now, surely.'

'So it will,' said Flora, smiling. 'Such fun for you.'

Suddenly a terrible noise broke out in the kitchen behind them. The Starkadders were quarrelling again. But Flora never knew what it was about. She walked to her room, undressed and fell into bed, already half asleep.

9

Seth's departure

The next day was Sunday, so fortunately everybody could stay in bed and get over the shocks of the night before. At least, that is what most families would have done. But the Starkadders were not like most families. Life burned in them with a fiercer flame, and by seven o'clock most of them were up, and, to a certain extent, working.

Reuben, of course, had a lot to do because of Amos's sudden departure, and was delighted to be in charge of the farm. The five Starkadder wives had been accompanied back to the village by Adam, at half-past five that morning, and the old man had returned in time to begin the milking. He was still confused by the news of Elfine's engagement, and did not notice that Aimless had lost a foot.

It was a beautiful spring day, with birds singing in the trees. Judith sat, grey-faced, in the kitchen, looking out with dull, miserable eyes over the green countryside. Rennet stayed by the fire, stirring some rather nasty soup she was making. She had decided to stay at the farmhouse when the other female Starkadders had departed with Adam; she did not want their unspoken pity.

Old Ada Doom stayed in her room, where she had been carried at six o'clock that morning by Micah, Seth, Mark, Caraway, and Harkaway. No one dared go in to see her. She sat alone, a bent, ugly ruin of a woman, staring unseeingly into the distance. Her fingers picked endlessly at the *Milk Producers' Weekly*. She did not notice the sharp blue air of spring outside. Powerless waves of anger flooded her ancient body, and sometimes names burst from her green lips. 'Amos ... Elfine ... Urk ...'

No one had seen anything of Urk since he had gone rushing out into the night carrying Meriam, the hired girl. It was generally assumed that he had drowned her and then himself. Who cared, anyway?

As for Flora, she was still asleep at half-past three in the afternoon, and would have continued sleeping comfortably enough until teatime, but she was woken by a knocking at her door.

'Two gentlemen to see you, Miss Poste,' Mrs Beetle was saying excitedly.

'Oh, who are they? Have they told you their names?' asked Flora sleepily.

'One's that Mr Mybug, miss, and the other's a gentleman who says his name's Neck.'

'Oh yes ... of course, how delightful. Ask them both to wait downstairs till I come. I won't take long,' and Flora began to get dressed. She was delighted at the idea of seeing her old friend Mr Neck again. Of course, Mr Mybug was a nuisance, but she could deal with him easily enough.

She went downstairs at last, looking as fresh as a leaf, and as she entered the kitchen, Mr Neck came forward to greet her, holding out both his hands and saying, 'Well, well, sweetheart. How's the girl?'

'I am fine, Earl,' said Flora warmly.

Mr Mybug, who had hoped to find Flora alone, was looking annoyed. He became even more annoyed when he heard Mr Neck call Flora 'sweetheart', but after a while he decided that Mr Neck must be the sort of Amusing Type who calls everybody 'sweetheart', and did not mind so much.

Flora instructed Mrs Beetle to make them some tea, and they sat very pleasantly in the sunshine which poured in through the window, drinking their tea and talking. Flora felt sleepy and relaxed. She had made up her mind that Mr Neck must not go without seeing Seth, and quietly told Mrs Beetle to find him and send him to the kitchen as soon as possible.

'Have you come to England to look for film stars, Mr Neck?' asked Mr Mybug, eating a little cake that Flora had wanted for herself.

'Yeah, that's right. I want to find another Clark Gable. You wouldn't remember him, maybe. A great film actor, twenty years ago. I want someone like him, a big good-looking man who smells of the countryside, with a golden voice. I want passion. I want red blood. I don't want any delicate sensitive types, see? The great American public have had enough of them.'

'Do you know the work of Limf?' asked Mr Mybug eagerly. 'One of the greatest of our modern film-makers, I always think. Difficult, of course. But *real!*'

'Never heard of him,' said Mr Neck, who had decided that he did not like Mr Mybug. 'Thank you, sweetheart,' (to Flora, who was feeding him cake). 'You know, Mr Mybug, we gotta responsibility to the public. We gotta give them what they want.'

He paused and drank his tea. The sunshine played on his little, lined, monkeyish face and on the fresh flower he always wore in his buttonhole. 'I want a man to appeal to the women,' he continued. 'Someone who can look good in evening clothes, but ride a horse and dig a field as well. I gotta find somebody.'

'Have you seen Pepin's latest film?' asked Mr Mybug. 'I saw it in Paris last January. Very amusing and – er – modern.'

'I saw it in Paris too,' said Mr Neck. 'It gave me a pain. Gave me a lot of new ideas as well. How *not* to make a film. I've met Pepin too. The poor man's mad.'

'He is much admired by the younger men,' said Mr Mybug daringly, with a glance at Flora for approval.

'That helps a lot,' said Mr Neck bitterly.

While he was speaking, Seth had come silently to the kitchen door. He now stood there, looking down enquiringly at Flora. She smiled across to him. Mr Neck's back was towards the door, so he could not see Seth, but when he saw Flora smile he turned half round, and looked across at the doorway.

And he saw Seth.

A silence fell. The young man stood in the warm light of the dying sun, his bare throat and handsome face looking as though they were painted gold. Relaxed and self-confident, like any healthy animal, he looked just what he was – the kind of man who breaks the hearts of women for miles around. Millions of women would realize, in the next five years, that Seth could be imagined anywhere, in a country village, in a seaside town, in a busy city, and he would still remain for ever the lover whom women could not resist, and for whom they would gladly give up home and duty for a moment of passion.

Was it surprising, then, that Mr Neck broke the silence by

throwing up his hand and saying in a broken whisper, 'That's it, sweetheart! That's got it! Hold it!'

And Seth was so familiar with the language of films that he obeyed, staying completely still for another second or two in silence.

'That's it, sweetheart! That's got it! Hold it!'

Then Flora said, 'Oh, Seth, I wanted Mr Neck to see you. Earl, this is my cousin, Seth Starkadder. He's very interested in films. Mr Neck makes films, Seth.'

Mr Neck, forgetting everything else, was leaning forward with his head slightly bent, to hear Seth speak. And when that deep, warm voice said slowly, 'Pleased to meet you, Mr Neck' – Mr Neck looked up with an expression of extreme relief and delight.

'Well, well,' said Mr Neck, 'so how's the boy? You and I must get to know each other, right? Maybe you'd thought of doing some acting yourself?'

Mr Mybug sat comfortably back in his chair and put a little cake in his mouth. He was looking forward to seeing Mr Neck make fun of Seth. Seth himself was looking angry; he was not sure how sincere this American was.

'No, no, I'm not joking,' said Mr Neck quickly. 'I mean it. Would you like to act in a film?'

A great cry broke from Seth. Mr Mybug fell off his chair, and swallowed too much cake. No one noticed him. All eyes were on Seth. His eyes shone, as he answered slowly, 'More than anythin' else in th' world.'

'Well, isn't that great?' said Mr Neck, looking round proudly for agreement and support. 'He wants to be a film star and I want to make him one. Now, sweetheart, get your bags and we'll catch a plane to America tonight. But what about your family? Will they agree?'

'I'll tell you all about that, Earl,' said Flora. 'Seth, go and pack what you need for the journey.' And when Seth had gone silently out, she explained the situation to Mr Neck.

'So it's all right if Grandmother doesn't stop us?' said Mr

Neck. 'Well, we must leave quietly, that's all. Tell her not to worry. We'll send her five thousand pounds out of the first film he's in. Oh, he's fantastic! He's just what I want! It'd take more than anyone's grandmother to stop me now.'

When Seth returned, wearing his best hat and a coat, and carrying a suitcase, everybody moved towards the door. As they walked towards Mr Neck's car, which was waiting in the farmyard, Mr Neck held tightly on to Seth's arm, as though he feared Seth might change his mind. He need not have worried. The expression on Seth's face seemed to say, 'Of *course* I am going to be a film star. It's what I've always expected.' He was too proud to show the fierce joy deep inside him.

Well, everything was going beautifully, and they were all standing round the car saying goodbye, when suddenly they heard the alarming sound of a window being opened. A voice floated out into the quiet air of the late afternoon. It was observing that it had seen something nasty in the woodshed.

Everybody looked up, Flora a little worriedly. Sure enough, it was Aunt Ada Doom. She was leaning out of her bedroom window. Behind her left shoulder there was a shape, which, because of the untidiness of its hair, must be Judith. Another shape behind her right shoulder was probably Rennet.

'Oh dear!' whispered Flora rapidly to Mr Neck. 'Hurry up and go!'

'Is that Grandmother?' asked Mr Neck. 'Come on, sweetheart,' he added to Seth, 'we gotta catch a plane.'

'Seth . . . Seth . . . where are you going?' Judith's voice was full of terror and pain.

'I saw something nasty in the woodshed!' screamed Aunt Ada Doom, waving all that was left of the *Milk Producers' Weekly*.

'My baby . . . my darlin' Seth! You mustn't leave me! I shall go mad!'

'Seth . . . you mustn't go!' begged Judith. 'You can't leave your mother! And there's work to do!'

'I saw something in the woodshed!'

'Yes, but did it see you?' murmured Mr Neck, getting into the car beside Seth. The engine started and the car began to move out of the yard. 'I know it's hard,' he shouted up to Aunt Ada, with his head out of the car window, 'but that's life, girl. I respect a grandmother's feelings, sweetheart, but I just can't give him up. He'll send you five thousand out of the profits of his first film. That's a promise.'

'Goodbye,' said Seth to Flora, who smiled back at him in a friendly way. She watched the car drive away. Seth would never have a chance, now, of becoming a nice, normal young man. He would become a world-famous, swollen mask, smiling down from a great silver screen in dark cinemas. Already he was beginning to seem unreal.

Aunt Ada and Judith were still screaming and crying in the bedroom. But Rennet was now leaning out of the window, and Mr Mybug had noticed her. 'Who's that?' he asked Flora, in a low voice. Flora told him. 'What a fascinating face,' he said, staring up at Rennet. 'Delicate, nervous . . . She has that untamed look you see sometimes in newly born animals. Don't you feel it?'

Rennet was staring down at him, too. Flora could see they were attracted to each other. It would be quite a good thing if he married her and introduced her into his intellectual circle . . . except that she, Flora, must make quite sure that he would be a good husband to poor Rennet. He probably would be. Rennet could cook and clean and sew, so she would look after Mr Mybug, and love him very much, and he would become very comfortable, and would be very grateful to her.

Mr Mybug walked across the yard and called up to the window, 'I say! Will you come for a walk with me?'

'What . . . now?' asked Rennet shyly. Nobody had ever asked her to do such a thing before.

'Why not?' laughed Mr Mybug boyishly. Flora thought it *was* a pity he was rather fat. He was obviously very pleased with himself. Flora knew that intellectuals thought the proper – no, the only – way to fall in love with somebody was *instantly*.

Rennet left the window, and Flora suddenly felt extremely sleepy. Things were happening a little too fast at Cold Comfort. She wished Mr Mybug a pleasant walk with Rennet, and was on her way across the yard to the kitchen door, when Mr Mybug said, 'We're friends, aren't we?'

'Certainly,' she replied pleasantly.

'We might have dinner together in London sometime?'

'That would be delightful,' agreed Flora, thinking how nasty and boring it would be.

'There's something about you . . .' said Mr Mybug, staring at her and waving his fingers. 'Something distant . . . and pure. I'd like to write a novel about you, and call it *The White Goddess*.'

'Do, if it passes the time for you,' said Flora, 'and now I'm afraid I really must go. Goodbye.'

Later that afternoon, she was delighted to hear from the very useful Mrs Beetle that Elfine had been invited to stay at Hightree Hall for six weeks, and had already been collected by Dick in his car. It also appeared that Urk and Meriam were still alive, and planning to get married very soon; Mrs Beetle was determined to make sure that he looked after Meriam and all her children, the future jazz band, properly.

The final news of the day came on a postcard, which was delivered to the farmhouse after supper. It read:

Praise the Lord! This morning I preached the Lord's word to thousands in the market-place. I am now going to hire a Ford van. Praise the Lord! Send my cotton shirts. Fond love to all.

Amos Starkadder

10

Judith and Aunt Ada

After the departure of Seth, life at the farm returned to normal (at least, as normal as it ever was), and Flora was quite glad to have a rest after the exhausting weeks of training Elfine, and the exciting events which had removed Seth and Amos from Cold Comfort.

The first of May brought the summer weather. There were rich green leaves on all the trees, and the warm, soft air breathed love. Mrs Beetle appeared in a cotton dress, while Flora wore pale green and a shady hat.

But Judith lay on her bed in silence, and the sunshine did not warm her room. She had put a little piece of black cloth over each of the two hundred photographs of Seth, and now, what else did life hold for her? The flies flew around her room, with as much noise and as little meaning as life itself.

The old woman also stayed in her room, sitting in front of the fire, and talking to herself. Flames of hate lit her darkness. She felt the summer was taking away all the Starkadders from Cold Comfort. Where was Amos? The sunlight answered. Where was Elfine? The birds sang in reply. Where – worst of all – was Seth? She did not even know where he had gone or why. Was everyone mad, except her, sitting alone, an ancient body in front of a fire? And Urk, a Starkadder, saying he was going to marry the girl paid to work in the kitchen . . . It was Robert Poste's child who had done this, who had poured poison into the ears of the family, and sent them out into the world. They would all go – Judith, Micah, Ezra, Harkaway, Caraway, Luke, Mark . . . Then . . . when they had all gone . . . she would be alone at last – alone in the woodshed.

Flora was having quite a nice time. It was now the second week in May, and the weather was still wonderful. As everybody now considered Reuben the owner of Cold Comfort, he had started making improvements to the farm, and asked Flora if she would accompany him into Godmere, to help him choose some new equipment. So one Wednesday morning, they drove off together in the horse and trap, and after a busy morning shopping, had lunch at the Red Lion Hotel.

'Where did you get the money to buy all those lovely tools, Reuben?' asked Flora, as she ate her chicken.

'I stole it,' replied Reuben simply.

'Who from?' asked Flora, who was bored by having to pretend to be shocked at things, and really wanted to know.

'From Grandmother. Ye see, I put false information in th' accounts. When we sell twelve eggs, I write down two, see? And I keep the money from the rest. She checks th' accounts twice a week, but she hasn't noticed yet. I've been doin' it for nearly five years – I've been planning this, see?'

'My dear, I think you're *so clever*,' said Flora. '*Quite* amazing. If you continue like this, the farm will make *lots* of money.'

'Aye, if th' old devil doesn't change his mind and come back from America,' said Reuben doubtfully.

'Oh, I'm sure he won't,' said Flora decidedly. And she produced from her handbag, for the tenth time that morning, a second postcard, which said:

Praise the Lord! I go to spread the Lord's word among the godless Americans. Praise the Lord! Tell Reuben he can have the old place. Send clean underwear. Love to all.

Amos Starkadder

'Yes, I'm sure he means it,' repeated Flora. 'I wouldn't worry if I were you.' So they finished their meal in comfort. Just as Reuben was wiping his lips, he stopped and said, looking across at Flora, 'I don't suppose 'ee would marry me, Cousin Flora?'

Flora was much moved. She had grown to like Reuben in the last fortnight. He was worth whole sackfuls of the other male Starkadders. He was really very nice, and kind too, and ready to learn from anyone who could help him improve the condition of the farm. He had never forgotten that it was Flora who had suggested to Amos that he should go on a preaching tour, and he was deeply grateful.

She put out her hand across the table. Wonderingly, Reuben took it and stared down at it.

'Oh, Reuben, that *is* nice of you. But I'm afraid I am not at all the kind of person to make a good wife for a farmer.'

'I like your pretty ways,' said Reuben.

'That's charming of you. I like yours, too. But honestly, somebody like Nancy from the village would be much better, and more useful on the farm, too.'

'Aye,' said Reuben slowly, after a pause. 'Maybe you're right. Nancy would be a good wife.' And he released her hand. He did not seem at all offended or hurt, and they drove home together afterwards in comfortable silence.

Elfine was still staying with the Hawk-Monitors, and Flora had twice been invited to tea there. Much to Flora's relief, Mrs Hawk-Monitor seemed very fond of Elfine, and described her to Flora as 'a dear little thing'. Flora congratulated Elfine in private.

The wedding was arranged for the fourteenth of June. Dick's mother had decided it should take place in Howling church, which was very beautiful. She then shocked Flora by suggesting that the reception should be held at Cold Comfort.

'So much more convenient than coming all the way back to Hightree Hall, don't you think, Miss Poste?'

'Oh, I say,' said Flora nervously, 'I rather doubt if that would work, you know. I mean, old Mrs Starkadder is – er – not very well. The – er – noise might upset her.'

'She could stay in her room. A tray of cake can be taken up to her. Yes, I think that would certainly be the best thing. Is there a really *large* room at the farmhouse, Miss Poste?'

'Several,' said Flora faintly, thinking about them.

'Excellent. I will write to old Mrs Starkadder tonight.'

So there was a new horror on the horizon! Really, thought Flora, there was no end to her worries. She was beginning to think she would never be able to finish tidying up the farm in her lifetime.

However, it was true that matters were better since Reuben had taken over the management of the farm. Wages were paid regularly, rooms were cleaned, and accounts were kept correctly. Aunt Ada had not been downstairs since the night of the Counting, and the remaining male Starkadders, encouraged by the departure of Seth, Elfine, and Amos, had realized that she was only human. So they had brought their wives up to the farm, where they slept in rooms as far away from Aunt Ada's as possible. Life at the farmhouse was pleasanter for the Starkadders than it had ever been before, and they had Flora to thank for it.

But Flora was not satisfied. There was much still to do at Cold Comfort, before she could really say that the farmhouse was in a condition to satisfy Father Bertrand. There was the problem of Judith. There was old Adam. And then there was Aunt Ada Doom herself, the greatest problem of all.

She decided to start with Judith. After all, she had been lying in her room with the window shut quite long enough. Twice Mrs Beetle had asked if she could clean the room, and twice Flora had been forced to reply that it was not yet convenient. But now things had gone far enough, and when she arrived back at the farmhouse, she went straight up to Judith's room.

She knocked, but receiving no reply, went in. Judith was washing one of the two hundred little black curtains (for the two hundred photographs of Seth) in a bowl of water. Her eyes stared lifelessly out of her sorrowful face.

'Oh, Cousin Judith, would you care to come to London with me tomorrow?' asked Flora pleasantly. 'I want to do some shopping, and I hope to have lunch with a very charming friend of mine, a Dr Müdel from Vienna. Do come.'

Judith's bitter laugh shocked even the flies circling above her head into silence. 'I am a dead woman,' she said simply. 'Look . . . The little black curtain was dusty,' she murmured. 'I had to wash it.'

'I intend to catch the ten-thirty train,' said Flora patiently, 'and I will expect you to be ready by nine o'clock. You'll enjoy it, Cousin Judith. You mustn't carry on like this, you know. It – er – depresses us all terribly. And it's a pity to waste all this lovely weather.'

'I myself am a waste,' said Judith coldly. 'I am a used gourd . . . a skin. What use am I . . . now he's gone?'

'I myself am a waste. I am a used gourd . . . a skin.'

102

'Well, never mind that now,' said Flora comfortingly. 'Just be ready by nine o'clock tomorrow.' And after leaving Judith she sent Adam into Howling with the following telegram:

DOCTOR ADOLF MÜDEL

INTERESTING CASE FOR YOU. CAN YOU GIVE TWO OF US LUNCH AT GRIMALDI'S 1.15 TOMORROW WEDNESDAY.

LOVE F. POSTE

And that evening, while she was writing a letter to Charles, a telegram was delivered to her. It read:

BUT OF COURSE DELIGHTED. LOOKING FORWARD TO SEEING YOU. WHAT LOVELY WEATHER. ADOLF

The day in London was a complete success. True, it was a little awkward travelling by train with Judith, as she kept referring to herself wildly as a Used Gourd and a Skin, to the great interest of the other passengers. So it was a great relief to Flora to watch Dr Müdel take control of the situation. As a psychoanalyst, it was his job to help patients return to normal as far as possible, by encouraging them to concentrate on a new area of interest. During lunch at the Italian restaurant, Grimaldi's, Dr Müdel made what seemed like ordinary conversation with Judith. But Flora could see that he was skilfully encouraging her to talk about herself, and take an interest in something other than Seth.

'She will be all right now,' he whispered to Flora, when lunch was over, while Judith was staring moodily out of the window at the busy street below. 'I shall take her home with me, for a complete rest. She will stay for six months perhaps, with some of my other patients. Then I shall send her abroad. I think I will interest her in old churches. There are so many ancient churches in Europe that it will take her the rest of her life to see them all.

You see, Flora, all that energy – she was destroying herself with it. Now she can spend her energy on old churches – yes, yes, she will be all right.'

Certainly Judith was looking happier already and she clearly found Dr Müdel very sympathetic.

'I understand that you are going to stay with Dr Müdel for a while, Cousin Judith?' Flora said, while the Doctor was paying for the lunch.

'He has asked me. He is very kind . . . There is a dark force in him,' replied Judith. 'It beats . . . like a black bell. I wonder you do not feel it.'

'Oh, well, we can't all be lucky,' said Flora. 'But I think it's an excellent idea for you to have a holiday. It will do you good.'

She said goodbye to Judith there and then, and promised to send a share of the farm profits to her regularly, to pay for her pleasures during the next six months.

It was with a feeling of satisfaction, and something strangely like affection, that Flora returned, alone, to Cold Comfort that night. It was a mild and lovely evening, with no clouds in the sky. The farmhouse no longer looked dirty and miserable and depressing, as it had when she first saw it, several months ago. The windows were clean, with fresh curtains, and the farmyard smelt of the flowers Ezra had planted in the garden. Flora leaned forward, thinking, '*I* did all that.' And a feeling of joy opened inside her like a flower.

But then she looked upwards at the closed window just above the kitchen door. Aunt Ada was still in that room upstairs, fighting her losing battle. Could she, Flora, really congratulate herself upon her work at the farm, while Aunt Ada was still undefeated?

In the next few days, Flora was busy with preparations for Elfine's wedding reception. Reuben gladly gave her thirty pounds to pay for flowers and food. She went to London several times, to have a new dress made for herself. She also instructed the female Starkadders to clean every corner of the farmhouse; it was the first real cleaning it had received for a hundred years. Meanwhile, she kept an eye on the relationship between Mr Mybug and Rennet, and was relieved to hear that they were getting married in London, several days before Elfine, and attending the reception at Cold Comfort as a married couple.

As the evenings grew longer, Flora used to sit in a quiet corner of the kitchen, reading *The Higher Common Sense*, and hoping that Father Bertrand would provide the solution to the problem of Aunt Ada. And on an evening of more than usual peace and beauty, the answer came, suddenly, in a flash. In a few seconds she had every detail of her plan clearly in her head. Calmly she wrote a telegram to Claud Hart-Harris, asking him to send her the latest number of a particular fashion magazine, and a brochure for the Hotel Miramar in Paris.

Claud did not fail her. The papers were delivered the next day. Flora brushed her hair, and put on a fresh dress, and, as it was lunch-time, asked Mrs Beetle to give her the tray upon which was arranged Aunt Ada's lunch.

'Oh, no, miss, it's far too heavy,' said Mrs Beetle.

But Flora quietly took the tray, and, watched with fascination by Reuben, Mrs Beetle, and the female Starkadders, she put the magazine and the brochure on it. 'I am taking lunch up to Aunt Ada,' she announced. 'If I am not down by three o'clock, Mrs Beetle, will you kindly bring up some fruit juice. At half-past four you may bring up tea and cake. If I am not down by seven, please bring up a tray with supper for two, and we will have hot milk at ten. Now, goodbye, all of you. I beg of you not to worry. All will be well.'

And slowly Flora went upstairs, carrying the tray. They heard her knocking on the bedroom door and calling, 'May I come in, Aunt Ada? It is Flora.' There was a silence, then the door opened, and Flora and the tray entered. That was the last anyone saw or heard of her for nearly nine hours.

At three, half-past four, and seven o'clock Mrs Beetle took up the food and drink as instructed. Each time she could hear the steady rise and fall of voices inside, but although she listened for many minutes she could not distinguish a word, and this disappointing information was all she could carry back to the eagerly waiting group downstairs. Mr Mybug and Rennet had joined the Starkadders, and they all had a very pleasant evening, eating supper and talking about the farm and the family, past and present. Slowly it grew dark and cooler outside, and the summer stars came out.

Suddenly, at a quarter past ten, Mrs Beetle jumped up, saying, 'There! I forgot to take up the hot milk! I'll do it now.' But just then they all heard a light step on the stairs, and through the dark doorway walked Flora . . . at last. She looked calm, but rather pale and sleepy.

'Hullo,' she said pleasantly, 'you're all here, then? I'll drink that milk down here, Mrs Beetle. You needn't take any up to Aunt Ada. I've put her to bed. She's asleep.'

There was a gasp of wonder from everybody. Flora sank into her chair, with a long yawn.

'We were afraid for ye, dear soul,' said Reuben.

'Too nice of you,' said Flora sleepily. 'But it was quite all right,

106

really. You needn't worry – there will be no fuss at the wedding or anything. We've arranged everything.'

'Cousin Flora, nobody but 'ee could have done it,' said Reuben simply. 'How – how was it done?'

'Well, it's a long story, you know. We talked for hours. You'll see when the time comes. On the wedding day, I mean. You wait. It'll be a surprise. I can't tell you now. It would spoil things. It will be simply lovely. Surprise!'

Her voice had been growing sleepier and sleepier, and the glass fell from her hand. She was asleep.

'Just like a little, tired child,' said Mr Mybug, who like most daring intellectuals was as soft as cheese underneath, and he was just reaching out to stroke Flora's hair when Mrs Beetle smacked his hand, crying, 'Hands off, you!' This upset him so much that he and Rennet departed rather suddenly, without saying goodbye.

Mrs Beetle gently woke Flora, who stood up sleepily and smiled at Reuben as he gave her a candle.

'Good night, Cousin Flora. 'Twas a good day for Cold Comfort when 'ee came here,' he said.

'My dear soul, don't mention it. It's been such fun for me,' said Flora. 'Mrs Beetle, you know how I dislike making complaints, but the meat we had for supper was slightly undercooked. Mrs Starkadder's, in fact, was almost *raw*.'

'I'm sorry, I'm sure, Miss Poste,' said Mrs Beetle.

And then everybody went sleepily up to bed.

11

Elfine's wedding

The Starkadders were all at work very early on the morning of the wedding. The future jazz band were out picking flowers for the church and the farmhouse. The female Starkadders were making cakes in the kitchen, while Micah was putting the wine into buckets of ice, to keep it cool. Mrs Beetle and Flora were unpacking the silver knives, forks and spoons Flora had ordered from London. Chairs and tables were moved, bread was baked, flowers were arranged in vases, and at half-past eight everybody sat down to breakfast.

'I'll just take up th' old lady's breakfast,' said Mrs Beetle. 'There's some cold meat an'—'

'Oh, I've just been in to see her,' said Flora. 'She doesn't want anything except a 'Hell's Special'. Here, give me an egg. I'll mix it for her.' And they all watched in amazement as she beat a raw egg, some brandy, milk, and ice in a cup, and gave it to Mrs Beetle to take up to Aunt Ada.

'Will she come down an' upset everything after all, do 'ee think, Cousin Flora?' asked Reuben anxiously.

'Certainly not,' said Flora. 'Everything will be all right. Remember, I told you there was going to be a surprise. Well, it's just beginning.' And the Starkadders were satisfied.

They all worked enthusiastically for the rest of the morning. By eleven o'clock everything was ready, and as Flora looked round at the kitchen, with its vases of sweet-smelling flowers and its tables loaded with delicious-looking food, she was completely content. She went upstairs to visit Aunt Ada for a short time, shutting the bedroom door carefully behind her, and then went to her own room to wash and put on her new dress. Soon she came out, looking calm, happy, and elegant, ready for the pleasures of the day.

She and the Starkadders, all dressed in their best clothes, walked in the bright summer sunshine to Howling church, where they found quite a crowd of people already gathered. As soon as the female Starkadders sat down, they started to cry, but fortunately Flora had brought five spare clean handkerchiefs, which she passed silently along the row to them. She took a quick glance around the church; there the Starkadders were, enjoying themselves in an ordinary human manner, like normal people. Really, thought Flora, when she thought what they had been like, only five months ago . . . She bowed her head. She had achieved a great task, and had much to be thankful for. And today would see her greatest achievement of all!

At last! Everybody had turned towards the door of the church. 'Here comes the bride!' The low murmur ran along the rows, as a large car stopped at the door and the crowd outside started cheering. There was Elfine, pale and serious, floating into the church like a cool, white cloud. There was Dick, his pleasant red face betraying none of his nervousness, and his mother, in a grey suit. The ceremony was about to begin.

Half an hour later, the wedding was over, and Flora realized,

109

as she smilingly watched the best man, Ralph Pent-Hartigan, kiss the bride and congratulate Dick, how relieved and happy she was. She led the guests back to the farm, and very soon they were all entering the kitchen at Cold Comfort. Flora went in first, and stepped to one side, to let the guests have a clear view of the kitchen, and of somebody who rose from a chair, greeting them with the cry, 'So here you all are! Welcome to Cold Comfort!' It was a handsome old lady, dressed from head to foot in the most elegant flying suit of black leather, who came forward to meet her family and visitors.

''Tes Aunt Ada! 'Tes Aunt Ada Doom!' shouted Micah.

And the others, released from their first frozen shock of surprise, also broke into cries of amazement.

'Why, so 'tes! 'Tes terrible! 'Tes going against nature!'

'Aye . . . and in trousers, too! Do 'ee see 'em, my dear soul?'

'The first time in twenty years . . . 'Tes enough to kill her!'

'How delightful . . . so unexpected. How do you do, Miss Doom . . . or should I say Mrs Starkadder? . . . so confusing.'

'Oh, *Grandmother!*'

Aunt Ada stood in smiling silence while the shouting gradually calmed down. At last she held up her hand for silence. 'Well, good people, this is all very nice of you, but I think we must hurry up and begin the wedding reception, because I am leaving for Paris by air in less than half an hour.'

There was confusion again as the Starkadders expressed their shocked surprise at the suddenness of this change in Aunt Ada's character and routine. Flora realized that nothing but a good deal of food could persuade them to be quiet, so she and Ralph (she was beginning to approve of that young man) began to move around the crowd, persuading everybody to sit down and eat.

Then Elfine, gently urged by Flora, cut the wedding cake, and the party officially began.

Soon they were all enjoying themselves hugely. The shock of

''Tes Aunt Ada! 'Tes Aunt Ada Doom!' 'Aye . . . and in trousers, too!'

Aunt Ada's appearance gave everybody something to talk about, and only added to the delicious flavours of the food they were eating. After she had said a few pleasant words to all the guests, Aunt Ada sat down again, to drink some wine and eat a little. Flora sat beside her. She thought it was best to keep an eye on Aunt Ada until the last minute. The plane that would take Aunt Ada to Paris would be landing in one of the fields in half an hour. It seemed that Aunt Ada had thoroughly realized what a nasty time she had had for twenty years, and was now determined to have a nice one. 'But you never know,' thought Flora.

Flora was also waiting for the opportunity to ask her aunt about her mysterious rights, mentioned in Judith's letter nearly six months ago. Soon the moment came.

Aunt Ada thanked Flora for the hundredth time, for showing her what a pleasant time could be had in this world by a handsome, sensible old lady of good fortune, excellent health, and firm character. 'I am greatly looking forward to staying at the Hotel Miramar,' she added. 'Is there anything I can bring back from Paris for you, my dear?'

'A sewing-box, please,' said Flora. 'But Aunt Ada, there is something else I would like to ask you. What was the wrong that Amos did to my father? And what are my "rights" of which Judith used to speak? I feel I cannot let you go on your tour without asking you.'

Aunt Ada's face became serious. She glanced round the kitchen, and observed with satisfaction that everybody was eating much too hard and talking much too fast to take any notice of anyone else. So she leaned towards Flora and began to whisper into Flora's ear. At last the murmur stopped. Flora asked, 'And did the sheep die?'

But at that moment Elfine and Dick came to speak to Aunt Ada, and Flora's question went unheard.

'Grandmother,' said Elfine, 'Adam wants to come and live at Hightree Hall with us and look after our cows. May he?'

'Of course, my dear,' said Aunt Ada generously. 'But what will happen to Pointless, Aimless, Hopeless, and Careless if he deserts them?'

A wild scream broke from Adam. He threw himself forward, his ancient hands held together in pain. 'Nay, never say that, Mrs Starkadder. I'll take 'em wi' me. There's room for us all at Hightree Hall.'

'Well, well, you may take them if you want to,' said Aunt Ada, smiling.

Adam hurried joyfully away to tell the dumb creatures the good news, and Flora repeated her question, a little louder this time. She was anxious to know.

'And did the sheep die? And what about my rights?'

But it was no use. Mrs Hawk-Monitor chose that second to come up to Aunt Ada, to invite her to dinner at Hightree Hall as soon as her world tour had ended. So Flora's question was not answered, and would never be answered, because the next interruption was the noise of a plane approaching.

Everyone rushed out across the yard and into the big field behind the house. The pilot, a cross-looking young man, was presented with a piece of wedding cake, to his obvious disgust. Aunt Ada said goodbye to her family and guests, and thanked Flora again for all she had done to change her aunt's life. Flora smiled prettily, but could not help feeling a bit disappointed about the sheep and the rights. Aunt Ada climbed in, and the machine rose slowly from the ground. The crowd saw Aunt

Ada's confident face smiling down at them, as she was carried from their sight high into the sky.

'Now let's go back and drink some more wine,' suggested Ralph Pent-Hartigan, taking Flora's hand in a familiar but rather pleasing way. But Flora had to go and help Elfine change her clothes, as the newly married couple were also leaving by plane, in another half hour.

Elfine was very happy and not at all tearful or nervous about her new life. She kissed Flora and thanked her warmly for all her kindness and good advice. Flora gave her a copy of *The Higher Common Sense*, with a suitable message written inside the cover.

After Elfine and Dick's plane had taken them away, to the great excitement of the Starkadders, Flora began to feel very tired. She *was* so wishing everybody would go home. *And* she had forgotten to ask what it was that Aunt Ada saw in the woodshed. Now she would never know the answer to that question either.

Fortunately, the guests were leaving. Everybody, especially Mrs Hawk-Monitor, congratulated Flora on the deliciousness of the food and the elegance of the arrangements. She was invited to dinner at Hightree Hall, to coffee at the Mybugs' flat in London, and to tea with Urk and Meriam at the little house Urk had bought out of his profits from the water-vole business. She thanked them all smilingly, as she accepted.

One by one, the guests departed, and the Starkadders, sleepy with wine and the strangeness of enjoying themselves in a normal manner, crept off to their bedrooms for a rest. Mrs Beetle started tidying up in the kitchen.

'Miss Poste, you look exhausted,' said Ralph Pent-Hartigan. 'Come for a drive with me?'

'Thank you so much, but no,' said Flora. 'But could you possibly just take me down to the village? I want to telephone.'

He was delighted, and soon they were driving down the hill into Howling.

'I suppose you wouldn't care to have dinner with me in London tonight?' asked Ralph. 'It's a lovely evening. We could dance at the New River Club, if you like?'

'I would have loved it, but I'm afraid I've just decided to leave the farm tonight, so I'll be busy packing and so on. I'm so sorry. Some other time, perhaps.'

'Well, but . . . I could drive you back to London.'

The car stopped outside the phone box and Flora got out. 'Again, I'm so sorry,' she said, smiling into his disappointed young face, 'but I think my cousin is coming to fetch me. We made the arrangement months ago. I'm just going to see if he's at home.'

Luckily, she did not have to wait long in the phone box before Charles answered. 'Hullo,' said his quiet, deep, musical voice, many miles away.

Flora gave a little gasp.

'Oh . . . hullo, Charles. This is Flora. Look, are you doing anything tonight?'

'Not if you want me.'

'Well, could you possibly come and collect me from the farm in your plane? We've had a wedding here today, and I've tidied everything up. I mean, there's nothing left for me to do here. And I really am tired.'

'*I'm coming*,' said the deep voice. 'I'll be there at eight.'

There was a pause. 'Charles,' said Flora. 'It . . . I mean . . . it isn't too much trouble, is it?'

Smiling, she heard the distant sound of Charles's laughter.

Young Pent-Hartigan drove her back to the farm, before saying goodbye. She went into the house, where quiet was flowing back into the sunny empty rooms like the returning sea, and up to her bedroom. There she changed into a suit, and packed her bags, which would be sent to Mouse Place tomorrow. She was taking with her only *The Thoughts, The Higher Common Sense*, and a few things in a small case.

When she came downstairs again, the kitchen was tidy and empty, and all was cool, quiet and peaceful. Flora's supper was neatly laid on the table, and of the Starkadders there was not a sign. She supposed they must all be asleep upstairs, or mollocking in Godmere. She hoped they would not come downstairs before she left. She loved them all dearly, but this evening she just did not want to see them any more.

She sat down, with a contented sigh, to eat her supper. When she had finished, she wrote an affectionate little letter to Reuben, explaining that now her work at the farm was finished, she was returning to London, and promising to come back very soon and see them all. Then she put on her coat, picked up her case and went out into the cool evening.

It was the loveliest hour of the day. There was not a breath of wind, and the long, fresh grass in the field threw millions of shadows, which were growing steadily longer. Flowers were beginning to close, but their perfume still hung in the cool air. The sun was sinking behind the trees, and the birds were singing their last song before nightfall.

The countryside was falling asleep, and Flora looked up into the darkening sky. She could hear the sound of a plane in the distance. It came closer, and there it was at last, landing in the field. The pilot got out and came across to meet her, running his hand through his black hair.

It was the purest happiness to see him. It was like meeting again a dearest friend whom one has loved for long years, and missed in silence. Flora went straight into his open arms, put hers round his neck, and kissed him with all her heart.

Soon Charles said, 'This is for ever, isn't it?'

And Flora whispered, 'For ever.'

It was nearly dark. The stars and moon were out. Flora and Charles sighed at last, looked at one another and laughed.

'Look here,' said Charles, 'I think we ought to go, darling. Mary's waiting for us at Mouse Place. What do you think? We can talk when we get there.'

'I don't mind,' said Flora. 'Charles, you do smell nice. Is it stuff you put on your hair, or what? Oh, it is nice to think how many years we've got to find out things like that! At least fifty years, I should think, wouldn't you, Charles?'

'I hope so, darling. Actually, I don't put anything on my hair. Oh, Flora, I'm glad I was born!'

He started checking the plane for the return journey, while Flora told him what she had been doing at Cold Comfort. Charles said sternly that he did not approve of people who interfered with other people's lives.

Flora heard this with delight.

'Shall I be allowed to interfere with yours?' she asked. Like all women of strong character, she loved it when someone gave her orders; it was so restful.

'No,' said Charles, smiling at her disrespectfully. 'Now, are you ready, my dearest darling? Oh, Flora, I'm so unbearably happy! I can't believe it's true.' He pulled her roughly into his arms and looked anxiously down into her face. 'It *is* true, isn't it? Say "I love you".'

And Flora, deeply moved, told him just how much she did.

They climbed into the plane and took off over the trees. Flora put her warm lips close to Charles's ear. 'I love you,' she repeated. He turned, and smiled into her eyes. She glanced for a moment at the soft blue of the cloudless night sky. Tomorrow would be a beautiful day.

SUSSEX DIALECT

WORDS OR SPELLINGS USED IN THE STORY

aye yes	**ye** you	**o'** of	**'tes** it is
nay no	**'ee** you	**i'** in	**'twas** it was
liddle little	**'un** him	**wi'** with	**'twill** it will
mun must	**'em** them		

th' the

an' and

–in' –ing, e.g. doin' (doing), darlin' (darling)

NON-EXISTENT WORDS INVENTED BY
STELLA GIBBONS TO REPRESENT SUSSEX DIALECT

cletter the dishes to wash up

mollocking having sex

scranletting ploughing (digging and turning over the earth in the fields)

sukebind a summer-flowering plant

GLOSSARY

ball a formal party for dancing

beetle a kind of insect, often large and black, with hard wing-cases

bellow *(v & n)* to make a deep loud noise (such as a bull makes)

best man a male friend or relative of a bridegroom who assists
him at his wedding

brassière underwear worn to support a woman's breasts

brochure an illustrated booklet, often used for advertising

the Brontës the sisters Anne, Charlotte, and Emily (famous
nineteenth-century novelists) and their brother Branwell (an
alcoholic)

bull an adult male cow

chaperone an older woman who accompanies a young unmarried
woman on social occasions

concert (in this story) a performance of classical music

damned condemned to hell after death

doom *(n)* death or a terrible fate

doomed *(adj)* certain to suffer a terrible fate

elegant attractive and pleasing in appearance or manner

Ford van a covered vehicle, with no side windows, used for
carrying goods or people (*Ford* is the name of a vehicle
manufacturing company)

foul dirty, bad, horrible

gentleman a man of good family and social position, usually rich

gotta *(informal American)* the spoken form of 'have got a' or
'have got to'

gourd a container made from the hard skin of a large dried fruit
(*a used gourd* is an idiom meaning 'something no longer useful
or needed')

intellectual *(n)* a person with excellent mental abilities who enjoys activities that further develop the mind (a description used ironically in this story)

the Lord God

Master a respectful title, used by servants to or about their employers

milk *(v)* to draw milk from cows

mop *(n)* (in this story) a piece of sponge or cloth attached to a wooden handle, used for washing dishes

moral *(adj)* good in character; following right and accepted standards of behaviour

novel *(n)* an invented story in prose, long enough to fill a complete book

Persuasion a famous nineteenth-century novel by Jane Austen

poetry *(n)* literature in verse or rhyming form; **poet** *(n)* a person who writes poetry

porridge a cereal cooked in water or milk and usually eaten hot for breakfast

preach to explain religious ideas, to teach about religion (usually, but not always, in church)

primitive uncivilized

psychoanalyst a person who treats mental patients by studying the workings of their minds

sealed fastened, closed (*My lips are sealed* is an idiom meaning 'I am determined to reveal nothing')

shed a small building used to store tools, wood, bicycles, etc. or to shelter animals

shilling a British coin until 1971, worth 5p in today's money

sin *(n)* the offence of breaking religious or moral rules; **sinner** *(n)* a person who breaks these rules

style the distinctive way in which something is done or expressed

sweeping (of an arm movement or a statement) taking in a wide, vague area

sweetheart (an expression of affection) darling

task a piece of work which has to be done

telegram a message sent by telephone and delivered in printed form

thrilling causing excitement, full of emotional power

tidy up to put things in order

trap (horse and trap) a light carriage pulled by a horse

tray a flat piece of wood (or metal or plastic) with raised edges, used for carrying plates of food, cups of tea, etc.

water-vole a small animal, similar to a mouse, which lives in or near water

well *(n)* a hole dug in the ground so that water can be drawn up

windswept open to or swept by the wind

yeah *(American)* yes